A Case of Hometown Blues

A Case of Hometown Blues
A Mitch Malone Mystery – Book 3

By W.S. Gager

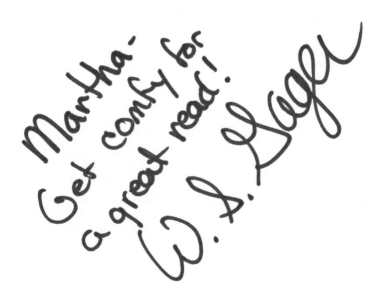

Martha-
Get comfy for
a great read!
W. S. Gager

Oak Tree Press   Taylorville, IL

Oak Tree Press

Oak Tree Press books may be purchased for educational, business or sales promotional purposes. Contact Publisher for quantity discounts.

First Edition, July 2011

Cover by Agrell Designs

Text Design by Linda W. Rigabee

ISBN 978-1-61009-017-9
LCCN 2011929385

Dedication

TO THE PEOPLE of Fremont, Michigan – Twenty years ago a young couple made their home there and you helped us raise two wonderful children. Thank you for all you did and the focus you placed on the arts and family. I wouldn't be published today without my great critique group. You are the best (and the turkey artichoke sandwiches didn't hurt!) I will miss so many of you. I wish there was space to list everyone. Fremont will always remain in our hearts as home!

To my mom—Who taught me how to juggle all the balls in life with grace and a smile, even while gritting my teeth. I still marvel at all you accomplish. Yet you always have time to drop everything and read when I need it and give me honest feedback. The writing retreats in Florida need to be an annual event!

Acknowledgement

TO RETIRED MICHIGAN State Police Post Commander Lt. Greg VanderKooi – Thank you for all your years of expertise and making sure my fictional police get it right. Any errors are purely my own.

Chapter 1

"HEY, MALONE. HOW can we expect to get a Pulitzer in this backwater?"

I wanted to roll my eyes. I had been nominated for the top prize in investigative journalism twice, but never won. My topic for this seminar to a sister newspaper's staff was finding big stories and working sources. However, Biff and Bob, I think that's what they said their names were, heckled me just for kicks.

This routine was familiar. I'd been known to do it when I was required to attend a seminar or two in the past. The rest of the afternoon was going to be painful, if I didn't stomp on these two and fast.

I didn't do painful. I was an award-winning journalist who covered the crime beat. I was immensely qualified to lead this seminar after receiving national headlines on a story in each of the last two years.

When a Mitch Malone exclusive ran, the advertisers ponyed up for weeks afterwards and circulation rose making my editor and publisher happy in a business that struggled to survive. I was asked to talk to other newspapers in the chain to encourage them to get bigger stories and edge the bottom line into black. I didn't like it, but didn't have a choice.

"When was the last time one of your stories made it on the wire?" I challenged the fresh-faced kid a couple of years out of college.

Bob looked at his shoes. Chair legs scraped against the floor as everyone in the room straightened their backs in the small conference room. I looked down the fake wood-grain table that had room for a couple more bodies. Now I had their attention and the sun pulled from behind a cloud and brightened the pale yellow walls.

"What makes a good story great and launches it into the wire services is the attention to detail. Not only creating a picture with your words, but using quotes to convey emotion. You have to work with your police departments, sources and your witnesses to have conversations with you in order to get at the depth of emotion in a story." I thought I had them now.

"Yeah, but what terrorists come to Flatville to train for a mission? You can see for miles." This from another irritant.

"Good and even great stories aren't found under rocks." Although I wanted to throw a few stones at the voice, I think was Biff. "Good stories are hard work and require investigation and talking to a lot of people, not just a single source."

I was back in control again. "I could have just gone with the double homicide story and moved on to the next burglary, but I wouldn't have been nominated for a Pulitzer for that. You have to develop a sense when something doesn't seem right. You need to push a little harder."

"You need to become wanted for murder and go into hiding."

This jeer was from Biff who obviously had done his research on me and my first big story about terrorists operating out of Grand River—the major metropolitan area where I lived and worked.

"I admit I had some incentive to figure out what was going on but the terrorist angle was the reason behind the killings. What made it a great story was the human-interest angle. The mother stood up to the terrorists at great personal loss while her husband was fighting for our country. She was getting intimidated and didn't back down and faced some pretty serious consequences. Making her the hero is what made it a great story. My involvement was never part of the story." I didn't have to tell them about Joey who was never mentioned but was the key to the whole episode.

"But nothing ever happens in Flatville." Bob was back in the tag team effort, a nasal whine in his voice.

"Nothing ever happens because you are not looking for it. You assume it doesn't exist. That is your first mistake." Anger tinged my words but I had had enough from these reporter wannabes. I would fire the lot of them if I were in charge.

"You think you're so good, can you find a story that makes it in the wire while you're in Flatville? You can't do it. I'll bet you can't." Biff nearly yelled the words, his face turning a motley-red color, a little spittle flying out to emphasize his point.

"You're challenging me?" I couldn't believe this had gotten so out of hand.

"Afraid you can't do it without all the big city crime to help?" Bob was not as angry but was backing up his coworker pushing me into a corner I didn't want to be in.

I looked around the conference table and six pairs of eyes were focused and intent. If I backed down, the rest of the seminars next week would be efforts in torture to get through and not accomplish anything. I also wouldn't be allowed out of the *Grand River Journal's* newsroom again.

"You want me to get a story that will run on the wire services before I leave at the end of next week?"

"That's what I said." Biff pounded the table.

"Fine. That should be easy. You obviously couldn't find a story if it bit you in the ass." With that parting shot I looked at the clock. My hour opening session on Friday afternoon was over. I turned on my heel and walked out.

What had I just done? I bet my whole career and credibility on getting a story. Not only that, but I only had a week to do it in a town I didn't know anymore. It took weeks and months to cultivate sources with the boys in blue.

I needed sustenance. Damn, I didn't even know where I could get a good cup of coffee and a passable doughnut. I was in trouble.

Chapter 2

THE BEER WAS cold. The place was dark. I could sit here and no one would know by my smell from the now smokeless bar that those morons at the newspaper had driven me to drink.

I took a big swallow and let the foamy coldness coat my throat. Nothing like a frosty mug on a ninety-degree day to sooth the nerves. I let the alcohol and air conditioning cool my temper. How could I have let the Mutt-and-Jeff team back me into a corner? How had I lost control? I shook my head and then caught myself in the mirror.

"Need another?" The bartender appeared in front of me

I looked up realizing he was asking about my beer and then down at my glass, surprised it was nothing but a little foam at the bottom.

"Sure."

The bartender moved down and I realized I needed to get something in me or I would be walking to my lodging. Good thing I'd already checked in before the seminar. It just tells you something about a small town when the proprietor of the only lodging in the town knows you because you lived next door to him while growing up. I didn't want to think about the possible lecture if their nearly-famous patron stumbled in soused.

The full mug appeared and I raised my hand to halt the bartender. "You got a menu around here?"

I expected a one page listing with everything fried or grilled. I was surprised by the menu's depth. Looking around to signal I was ready to order, I understood the larger selection. A ten-foot archway connected the bar with a banquet dining room. I opted for the burger basket.

I'm a connoisseur of hamburgers and had gotten the story of my life by finding the best hamburger place. Maybe this would be as lucky and I could easily hand Biff and Bob their egos when my byline appeared on their newspaper's front page. I wasn't supposed to be writing or reporting on this teaching expedition. Another long swig of aged hops disappeared as I kicked myself for foolishly falling into the reporting duo's trap.

My orders were simple. Instruct the staff on how to go beyond the available information to get to the why of the story. It was not simply about a traffic accident and who hit whom but about the people. Why was the woman going too fast? Was she late for work or was she rushing to the side of her dying grandmother only to end up beside her in a hospital bed? That is what made an okay story great. That is what built readership and that is what the *Flatville Gazette* needed to stay in business. Readers needed a reason to buy the paper and shop at advertisers who would pay.

Vowing to nurse the remaining half of my beer until the food came, I glanced around. The bar had started to fill up. Along the far wall the tables had been pulled together outside the banquet room. I wondered if it was a wedding reception. It looked like a pretty diverse group. Different pockets of people gathered, then rearranged themselves. People darted from group to group but they looked like they were having a good time. I turned back to my beer and realized I could easily watch them in the mirror behind the array of liquor bottles in tiered lines.

A blonde caught my eye as she flitted around. Her shoulder-length hair was straight and curled under as it hit her shoulders and seemed to glow in the dimly-lit room. She was reed thin from behind and wore a short, tight white skirt that showed a lot of leg and the leopard-print, sleeveless shirt was equally tight outlining a body that took work to maintain. She weaved her way to the bar.

I couldn't help myself. The back was impressive. I'd always liked blondes. I could remember one from high school who had never given me the time of day. She was a cheerleader and went out with the football player for most of our final two years. I turned in my chair to see what she looked like from the front.

I couldn't believe my eyes. I swiveled in my seat back to the bar and nearly upset my drink. As I cradled what was left of the brew, I realized I needed to quit drinking. I had just made the most popular girl from high school materialize beside me at the bar.

"Hey, Luke, how about another round?" She pointed to the table and made a circle with her finger. The front looked just as good although there were a few wrinkles around the eyes and mouth. She was the same girl who created wet dreams in my teens.

Luke, who was at the other end of the bar, must have given her the signal to wait and she did, her perfume smelled flowery and fresh wafting in my direction. Then I smelled something even better, burger. Luke set down my basket and I leaned in. This place might have to be a regular stop during my stay in Flatville. The fries were plentiful and golden brown. The aroma had me licking my lips. I leaned in and took a smell. Beef, grease and a hint of perfume. I was back in high school hell at the fast-food, burger joint in a booth wishing I had a driver's license.

Seeing my dream girl brought back what I had hoped never to remember. Flatville High School Class of 1996. It had been years since I had been "home during college." I didn't want to acknowledge it. This town had done nothing for me during my school years and it hadn't changed.

I didn't want to remember. I'd pushed it from my consciousness. It returned now.

The darkness. So much death. First my boyhood friend, Aaron, died and our trio of friends shattered. My parents tried to help. I was angry and just wanted to leave Flatville. I escaped to the university refusing to attend the one that employed my parents. They agreed but were disappointed.

They died. I returned only for the funeral. No one stepped forward to see what was going on with their only child. My uncle handled all the arrangements and I felt like the fifth cousin. I bailed after the funeral lunch was served, claiming I needed to get back for exams.

I refused to remember this part of my life. It was over, gone. The last time I was here I vowed never to return. My uncle never invited me for holidays and I never missed it.

I'd argued with my editor when we discussed my teaching mission to Flatville. I'd objected but I couldn't tell him it was my hometown and I didn't want to return. Then he would have wanted the whole sob story. No one knew my past and that's the way I liked it.

My editor wouldn't take no for an answer and I couldn't tell him I hated Flatville. I thought I could come back and pretend it was any other town. It wasn't. The baggage was still here. I couldn't run from it.

The town had forgotten me and I left them behind. Now I was back as the prize-winning gem in the newspaper chain giving others the benefit of my wisdom. I made a freshman mistake that had backed me into a corner and was going to force me into the streets in search of a passable story. I felt chased and haunted by memories.

"Damn."

"Your burger okay?" The bartender stopped to question as I realized I had spoken the last word aloud.

"No, I mean, yes, it's fine. What's up with that group?"

"Fifteen-year Flatville High School class reunion."

Luke turned back to other customers. I did some quick arithmetic and realized it was my class reunion. It had been fifteen years since I wore my cap and gown in this god-forsaken town. I didn't want anyone to know I was back. I hunched over my burger basket making quick work of it, intent on dodging classmates before someone recognized me.

"Mitch? Mitch Malone? Is that you?" The voice of my teenage dreams was just over my left shoulder. Time to tough it out and prove to this town I've left them behind. I was Mitch Malone, an award-winning reporter. I'd done something with my life. I glanced down at my now empty burger basket and hoped no condiments dripped on my button-down shirt. I swiveled my stool toward her voice and plastered a smile of happiness for the chance encounter.

"Trudy? Trudy Harrison? How are you?" I asked the question first hoping I would get a "fine" and she would move on.

My luck ran out. She shinnied onto the stool next to mine, grabbed my arm and started flapping her jaws at a rate of speed I couldn't keep up with. From her fifteen-minute diatribe I got she was married to an attorney who headed a company, divorced, no kids. She'd been in town for six months and was finding herself. Her ears glittered with karats and the former Mr. Right hadn't thought about a pre-nup. Trudy talked with her hands, arms flailing along behind. Had she done this in high school and I hadn't noticed? Was she nervous?

Then she stopped. Her mouth dropped open, then closed tight. Trudy stared over my shoulder and I wanted to turn and look, but before I could, I felt a large hulking presence sucking all the oxygen from the air.

My shoulders rounded, my stomach clenched. I didn't need to look to see who was behind me. It was the nightmare I thought I would have outgrown. It was the game-winning quarterback, the most popular guy in my high school. It was my cousin, Richard A. Malone Jr.

Chapter 3

"MITCHY. I HEARD you were in town." Ram—as he liked to be called—clamped his hand down hard on my shoulder and squeezed.

"Dick" — as I liked to call him — increased the pressure on my shoulder as I used the one nickname he could never stand and nodded in his direction. "Good news travels fast in a small town."

Trudy came off her stool and slunk up to her usual place in high school, draped all over Ram's shoulder but I had to appreciate her moves now. It forced him to let go of his iron grip.

"Ram," she said in her Marilyn Monroe knock-off voice. "Come see who's here." She pulled on his other arm and he was forced to let go of my shoulder as he followed her to the back table, which erupted in greetings to the town's hero.

I hated my cousin's nickname made from his initials. Within the span of thirty seconds, I had once again lost the girl and felt foolish. I was something now. I would show them. Mitch Malone was a force to be feared. Then I deflated.

My life couldn't get any worse. I had to find an award-winning story in the next seven days and the nemesis of my youth knew I was in town and would make my life hell, again. I couldn't win. I signaled the bartender for another mug.

I was halfway through drowning my sorrows when I checked my watch and realized it was close to nine o'clock. I looked over my shoulder and the crowd at the back including Ram and Trudy had added another dozen or so people and were laughing and carrying on. No one had bothered me. I figured it was time to get going while the going was good. I laid a bill on the counter to cover my charges.

Again, luck was not on my side. Biff and Bob bookended me on the bar stools to either side of mine.

"So this is how the great Mitch Malone gets his prize winning stories, drinking at the bar." Bob's tone was whiny and irritating.

"I'm off the clock. Even good reporters get some R and R. Beat it." I waved my hand in a dismissive gesture hoping they would get the hint.

"Is the great and powerful big-city cop reporter cranky because he knows he can't win his bet?" Biff chimed in making my head spin as I looked from one to the other. Shouldn't have had the third beer.

I'd had enough. I wasn't going to let these two wannabes get me. It was bad enough I had to suffer through Ram's humiliation. I wasn't going to take it from junior reporters. I was Mitch Malone, nominated for a Pulitzer. I was THE crime beat reporter at the *Grand River Journal*. Flatville was little more than a Podunk speck on the map.

"I not only can win this easy bet, the story will get picked up by a news service. Now beat it. I've got friends to see. I can wait to start until Monday. I'm that good!" I turned back to my beer and took a drink then started to stand, requiring Biff and Bob to move back and give me some room.

I did not want to stay at the bar and I wanted even less to go join my classmates chortling at the back of the room but the pair were more annoying at the moment. I could slink to the back and then cut out a side door or something.

Again my luck was all bad. The group magically opened enough for me to join. Cindy something, who I always thought of as Cindy Brady from the Brady Bunch because she wore her hair in pigtails and had larger than average front teeth, grabbed my attention.

"You're with a big paper aren't you? Whenever you have big stories the Flatville paper always runs your byline bigger than normal. That's how I know. They want people to think you started out here which is true if they think about where you grew up but you didn't work on the paper here, did you?"

I started to answer but she continued without waiting and I tuned her out. She always could talk, I belatedly wished I had continued for the nearest door. I glanced over my shoulder and Biff and Bob were still at the bar but had their own beers now and were watching me. I turned back to Cindy and pretended to listen to her monologue.

I looked over Cindy's head and caught Camelia staring at me. When our eyes locked she raised an eyebrow in question. I shrugged my shoulders. Camelia and I had had a math class together once. She wasn't good at math and always wanted my help. I think it was her second time through it and she passed thanks to my efforts.

Camelia always struck me as a person who wanted a better lot in life and would do anything to get it, but we were all kids then. She still looked fit and trim on her small frame.

"Mitch Malone. I thought you had blown this town vowing never to come back." Camelia's voice was low and sultry, a bedroom voice I had never realized in high school although it had been a lower timbre than most high-pitched girls.

"Me too. What are the odds I would be sent here from work at the same time as the fifteen-year reunion? I was never on the mailing list." I chuckled at my joke of being dropped from the list but Camelia only looked at me funny. No one ever got my humor back in high school either.

"Yeah, okay. Well, you look good. Married?"

I hated questions like this. I was not interested. Never was interested. Now they would be after me. Didn't they realize the man of mystery wasn't good marriage material? He was married to his career. He didn't like commitments of any kind. That's why he never returned to Flatville. No entanglements.

"No, not interested." Curt but I hoped she got the message.

"Oh, I see. I always wondered. You never did date." Camelia did a little up and down thing with her eyes and I realized she thought I was gay.

"No, no. Just too busy traveling to date. I like women." The words rushed out of my mouth. Flatville wasn't a politically-correct town and wouldn't tolerate differences and certainly not of a sexual persuasion. Any hint of deviance would be the butt of non-stop jokes and misery.

She stepped back with my outburst and then narrowed her eyes. Camelia appeared to take my words personally that I didn't want to date her specifically. Her eyes hardened vengefully, then it was gone.

"Oh, no. I wasn't interested," she said. "Just making conversation." She flapped her well-manicured nails at me. I wondered what color it was. Not purple but not pink either.

I dragged my eyes back to her face and realized she was watching something intently behind me. I turned. Ram wrapped an arm around Trudy's waist from behind and pulled her out of her conversation with a group of fellow cheerleaders, spun her around and layered her body against his using his hand on her butt to bring her in real close. She looked up at him bewildered and he never stopped his conversation or acknowledged what he did. I wasn't a big women's libber but that was just wrong on so many levels. I could see in Camelia's eyes that she thought so too.

Someone punched my other shoulder distracting me. It was Scott Nicewander. I inwardly cringed but held out my hand and pumped his enthusiastically. Scott, Aaron Oppenhizen and I became the three musketeers in fifth grade when old Mrs. Walkington could only keep track of her class if she put them in alphabetical order. Mrs. Walkington was a real crank but Scott, Aaron and I became thick as thieves discovering we didn't live far from each other. In Flatville, no one lived far from each other in a town that was an easy sprint from city limits to city limits.

I didn't want to talk about myself so my reporter instincts took over and I started to pepper Scott with questions to keep from discussing the darkest day of my youth.

"Hey, Scott, what are you doing these days?"

"I work at the hospital." Scott shrugged as if it was pretty lame.

"That's great. Married?"

"Divorced. You?"

"Never married. I like playing the field. Kids?" I laughed to show I was happy with my solitary existence.

"No. We weren't married long. Just didn't work." Scott shuffled his feet.

"Anyone I would know?"

He shook his head lowering it to his chest as if he had nothing to live for. I realized he had told me little info on himself. I was running out of questions.

I looked around for a way to escape but nothing materialized. I didn't want to talk to Scott. Our friendship had ended in the worst way and it wasn't something I wanted to remember. Being in Flatville was tough enough.

"Aaron would have loved this."

Damn. He had brought up my worst nightmare.

"Yeah." I couldn't think of anything to say. We both stared at our shoes wishing they would take us anywhere but here.

"Do you ever think about that day?" Scott persisted.

I backed up a step and scanned the crowd. No friendly faces or groups to join. I did not want to talk about Aaron. I had blocked it from my mind. It was how my family dealt with stress and difficulties. They locked it away and never discussed it.

I was a good boy and their only son. I tried to forget that Aaron ever existed and Scott followed. My days as a loner started with that terrible event.

Now I was face to face with Scott eighteen years later and I still couldn't face that day.

"I've had a lot of time to think."

I cut him off. "I don't want to think about it. Not here. Not now." I felt the panic begin. I turned my back on Scott unwilling to even examine or think about Aaron.

Trudy had slipped Dick's grip and was heading toward the bar. I took a chance and stepped forward to intercept her.

"Sugar, I need a drink." She pushed past me.

I followed her to the bar and turned to look at her.

"Gin and tonic."

I nodded to the bartender adding: "Draft."

I pulled out my money and peeled a twenty off and laid it on the bar. I looked at Trudy and knew she wouldn't be talking. She had a spacey look in her eyes that said she wasn't here.

The drinks made a thunk as they hit the bar. Faster than I thought possible Trudy grabbed the small tumbler and drained it in one tip of her pretty hand, long red nails glued to the glass like it was a lifeline.

"Take it easy." At this rate she would be laying on the floor in a half hour or puking.

Trudy set the empty glass on the bar and signaled for another. The bartender was moving a bit faster than necessary and within sixty seconds had another drink on the counter and I had removed a five from my cash stash to pay for it.

My mouth was dry and I took the first drink from my new mug.

"Sorry, Mitch." Trudy's reply was breathless. I looked down at her and locked eyes with the ones in my pubescent dreams. They were still beautiful but now had little lines of red running jagged maps to her soul.

"I drink too much at times." It was a flat statement. No denials of abuse, no blame laid on circumstances or other people. I liked it. I wondered if alcohol abuse was part of her self analysis. What had her life been like that she chose to leave and return to Flatville of all places? How much of a bigwig was her ex-husband and what company did he run? Did she return because it was the only place she had ever called home?

My reporter brain was spinning with questions and I wanted the answers. It had nothing to do with reacquainting myself with my school crush. There was a story here. I could feel it and I wasn't even thinking about Biff and Bob.

Chapter 4

"WHY DO YOU drink so much?" I suddenly wanted to help the girl from my dreams.

"Oh Mitch, I thought it would be easy if I could just get you here and now it's not. It's a lot of water under the bridge. I'm not strong enough, but I'm working on it." She saluted me with her glass and took a long gulp of the gin and tonic.

"Sometimes the truth will set you free." I gave her my best smile and tried to look like the comforting boy next door. The phrase was trite, old and probably untrue.

"Mitch, I wanted to tell you years ago when it happened." She looked uneasily over her shoulder at Ram.

"It's safer if I don't say anything. I see that now." She turned back and wouldn't meet my eyes as she drew the tumbler to her lips, her hands shaking and the fluid started to rim the edge as it hit her lips. She closed her eyes.

"You know that isn't true. You're giving someone too much power over you with your silence. Those schoolyard issues disappeared when we graduated." I cupped her elbow and gently squeezed. Trudy kept saying my name like it was either a lifeline that would save her or to remind herself whom she was talking to.

Her eyes opened and there were tears in them. "It's too late. You would hate me. It was so long ago. This town has too many secrets."

"It matters to you. Look at yourself." I pointed to the mirror above the bar. "You are shaking like a leaf. You deserve to be happy."

"No I don't. I thought if I told the truth it would make everything better but I see I would only be causing more pain." Her chin dropped to her chest and she twirled the ice in her glass and then took another gulp. "I sold my soul and I can't get it back."

"Why don't you let me be the judge of that?" She looked up and a single tear rolled down her cheek. I wanted to pull her close not just for comfort but to fulfill my youthful dreams.

"Mitch, you were always sweet."

A shadow fell over us and I looked up to see Ram. "You are messing with my best girl, Mitchy."

"I don't see a ring on her finger, Dick. You've had plenty of time. Maybe she's interested in a better Malone." The beer and Ram's draconian attitude lent me courage. "Back off."

Ram turned red, grabbed Trudy's arm, jerking her behind him.

"Leave her alone, pest. She ain't interested. She's my date."

"Still manhandling the women because they won't come willingly, huh Ram? It's time you grew up. The LADY hasn't said she was ready or interested." I tried to look around him to see Trudy but his bulk prevented it.

Ram reached back and I realized he meant to throw a punch. The bar had gone quiet, the patrons realizing something was going to happen. The arm started to move forward and it was like slow motion but I knew in my brain, fuzzy from one too many beers, I wasn't going to be able to duck in time.

Then the arm stopped and a sea of navy blocked my view. I shook my head to clear it and then the blue turned and my eyes traveled higher. Sam. Ram's partner in crime — the ace running back and Ram's favorite target on the state championship football team. I had been the pair's favorite target off the field. Sam, a police officer? Could things get any scarier?

"Take it easy, Ram. You can't get in a playground scuffle with your cousin now. He might just press charges being a big city celebrity and all." The last said with a mockery that was hard to miss.

My youth was coming back to haunt me. Scott was even at my side. "You don't want to challenge the police chief's authority. That's when

Sam Jones uses his force to get even. You don't want to be a guest in his hotel," he said under his breath.

My stomach sank. I certainly wouldn't be getting any exclusives in Flatville with Sam Jones on the force and certainly not with him being chief.

As if he had read my mind. "Mitch, Sam Jones, Flatville Police Chief. Seems you stirred up a heap of trouble. You should just return to your big city reporting. You will not be covering any crime exclusives while in Flatville."

That got my blood boiling. Sam and Ram had terrorized me in my youth. I was an adult now and not going to let it continue. "It's a free country. I can eat and drink where I please. I've done nothing illegal."

"Yet," Sam said.

Realizing I would be walking to my lodging, I couldn't let Sam get in the last word. "I'm the injured party. I was about to be assaulted."

"Anybody here see Mitchy boy being assaulted?"

Everyone who had been watching with interest suddenly turned from the scene or dropped their eyes. I was beginning to see a whole new side to Flatville. Maybe there was a story here and it had something to do with police brutality. I went into reporter mode.

"Can I quote you on that?" I reached behind and pulled my notebook from my back pocket, glad to see the pen still in its spine. "Sam Jones or do you go by Samuel now?" I didn't wait for him to answer.

"That would be Sam," he ground through his teeth.

"Chief of Police Samuel Jones did not get any witnesses to the assault on Grand River Police Reporter Mitch Malone currently on assignment in Flatville." I pretended to scribble myself the note knowing it wouldn't go anywhere but wanted to raise Sam's hackles. I now had some weight of my own to throw around when it was necessary.

I glanced at Ram who looked a bit deflated by Sam's reluctance to slap the cuffs on and haul me away. He hadn't outgrown his ability to solve problems with his fists. Then I noticed that the damsel in distress I had been standing up for was missing. I swiveled my head trying to make sure Trudy wasn't hidden behind Ram's bulk or in the crowd we had attracted with our raised voices. She had vanished.

"How about a couple of beers?" Sam's voice was loud distracting me from my search. Sam was still breaking the rules if he was drinking while on duty. Another angle for my exposé.

Odd, the bartender was missing. Maybe in the excitement he decided to get a little restocking done and make an early night of it. Ram slammed the flat of his hand on the bar with a loud whack. The bartender reappeared from the opposite end grabbing a mug, doing a quick swipe at the tap on his way and sliding it to Ram half filled with foam.

Ram didn't seem to notice the quality of his drink but took a large swig. More beer in Ram wouldn't help his disposition. Ram was mean, drunk or sober. Ram never forgot a slight or insult in my youth and payback was brutal. I didn't need any of that tonight. The party and happy reunion deflated. I didn't want to renew any more acquaintances. Ram and Sam were enough. The crowd had returned to their conversations and laughter. The spotlight of interest was gone and time to make my exit.

I slid out the front door taking a few breaths of the clean air. It was a beautiful night for a walk. The moon was full, the air was warm with a bit of a breeze and I was just a tad lightheaded from the adrenaline rush in the bar. My hotel, or rather a bed and breakfast, was only a few blocks away and I started in that direction.

I glanced over my shoulder making sure Ram hadn't followed to continue his treatment in the parking lot without any witnesses, when a ghostly image flitted across the back of the parking lot. I took deep breaths of air to clear my head. I really shouldn't have had the beer with Trudy because now I was seeing ghosts. Shaking my head, the image came into focus and it was the blonde hair and white skirt of Trudy reflected in the moonlight.

"Trudy?"

The figure startled and I could see her begin to shake.

I trotted over to her and grabbed her elbow. She'd been crying and her mascara had made deep black circles under her eyes.

"I just want to leave. Let me go," she stammered.

I looped my arm around her shoulder and she was icy to the touch. It was the middle of July and a heat wave refused to cool the humid air. We had reached a black Mazda Miata and she began fumbling in her purse.

After a few seconds she hauled out a set of car keys and promptly dropped them in the gravel.

I retrieved them and hit the unlock on the key fob realizing I was more sober than Trudy and I couldn't let her drive.

"Let me drive you home." I steered her to the passenger side, opened the door and when she didn't move, gently pushed her down so she had no option but to sit. I then swung her legs around and shut the door.

"I haven't finished. I need to tell him more. He was going to help me."

"Maybe tomorrow you can finish. Now you need sleep."

I heard music and realized someone had opened the bar door and was leaving.

Trudy looked and then shrank back so she wouldn't be seen. I increased my pace and hopped in the driver's side door, started up the sporty model and pulled out of the lot with more speed than was necessary but enjoying the feel of the engine's power.

"Thanks, Mitch. You were always a good sport." The voice was slurred and sounded close to passing out.

"Where you staying? Do you live in Flatville?" I was just driving and not sure I wanted to be out in the open and caught behind the wheel. It was easy to go too fast with the only two traffic lights blinking caution while the majority of town slept.

"Staying in town, just until I can get a few things cleaned up. Taking care of my dad. I hate this town."

"Where?"

"Mitch, I never thanked you for standing up for me in there."

"Trudy, where do I take you?"

"Ram told me what happened years ago and made me promise not to tell. Said I would go to jail."

She was rambling now.

"First time I've been back was six months ago. My mother died. Mistake. Now I can't leave. Too many problems."

"Where do you want me to take you?" I was sobering up fast.

"Anywhere but here. Here is so bad. Bad memories. Bad karma. Bad news."

I didn't know what to say so I sped out of town pumping the gas and enjoying the power under the hood as we left the city limits and Sam's jurisdiction heading for the next one-horse town that I thought still had a twenty-four-hour diner. Food would sober us up, but even then I wasn't sure she would make sense.

"I didn't do it Mitch." She sat up straight and grabbed my arm in a vise grip.

"Let go. You want to get us in an accident?" I swerved the wheel back onto the pavement just as the right tires were dropping down to the gravel.

"I didn't do it and no one can make me say I did."

"Okay, take it easy." I tried to pry her fingers loose by grabbing the wheel with the arm she had and using the other to pry her fingers loose. My fingers keeping us on the road were tingling from the lack of blood flow.

I found a McDonalds parking lot and knew I needed coffee. I parked and turned to face Trudy. With my full attention to her, I grabbed her hand and broke the grip. Little needles of pain sliced through and I resisted the urge to rub it.

"Trudy, I'm not saying you did anything wrong. I'm not even sure what we are talking about here."

"Aaron." She burst into tears hiding her face in her hands.

I had to have misunderstood. She couldn't be talking about Aaron Oppenhizen. He died more than eighteen years ago.

I didn't want to think about that. Couldn't think about. When Aaron died, I pretended he never existed. It was easier than face the guilt about being responsible for his death. Why did I agree to come to Flatville? First Scott, now Trudy trying to talk about Aaron.

Mitch Malone didn't look back. He didn't analyze his feelings.

He wouldn't, he couldn't.

Chapter 5

I TRIED TO get more cohesive information from Trudy but she had clammed up. The ride back to Flatville was quiet and I wasn't even sure she was awake. Her head was turned toward the window and she hadn't moved. I pulled up in front of her parent's house. Before I could even bring the car to a stop she was reaching for the door.

She was walking unsteadily up to the side door. I was making sure I'd turned the lights off and just savoring the feel of the sports car before exiting. I figured it would be easy to catch up to Trudy.

"Go away." Trudy had stopped in the shadow near the four cement steps that lead up to the side door and into the kitchen. I saw her hand come up and try and wave away a fly or something buzzing. I couldn't see anyone and wondered if she was hallucinating.

Then I heard a low voice and wondered if Ram was waiting for her and mad she had ditched him at the reunion.

"You have already bilked our father out of his house and stolen anything with a value to feed your habit. You will get nothing more." Trudy's voice got steadier the more she talked.

"I need money. I've got bills to pay, the note on the bar."

I was close enough now that I could see an outline of someone sitting on the steps.

"No, Kim. You've gotten all there is. There is nothing left. Dad needs care and now he can't pay for it."

I was beginning to understand the lines around Trudy's eyes. It was terrible when your parents were sick.

"I'll pay it all back with interest. Just this once, please?"

I could see Trudy weaving and I thought it was her considering it. "No. I'm sorry Kim but dad comes first. Find another way."

Kim jumped to his feet. "You've always been jealous of me. You just want all the money for yourself so you can go back to where you were and live the life of a society matron."

Trudy acted like she'd been slapped by the venom in the voice. "Go away," she screamed. Kim advanced on her and so did I.

"I think you better leave." I used my stern voice.

"Where'd you come from?"

"It doesn't matter. The lady asked you to leave." I straightened up as tall as possible so he would have to tilt up to see my face.

He stepped around Trudy and disappeared around the corner of the street. Trudy was shaking but I wasn't sure if it was cold, anger or nerves.

I lifted her hand and pressed the ring of car keys into it.

"Get a good night's sleep. It will look better in the morning." I nearly gasped aloud at the words I'd said. It was something my mother always said when I was stewing about a problem at school or in most cases with Ram.

"Thanks, Mitch." She climbed the first step and then turned. She planted her lips on my forehead. "Maybe we could meet in a day or so. I know you could help. You would know how to handle it. The gin was a bad idea." After a couple of tries she got the key in the lock and opened the door, disappearing inside.

I was on cloud nine. I'd finally kissed the homecoming queen. Okay she kissed me and not on the lips but it was special. This week might be more enjoyable than I thought. Maybe we could do dinner. I might give her a call tomorrow afternoon and see when we could get together.

I debated about going back to the bar to get my rental car but decided it could wait. My room at the bread and breakfast was a couple of blocks away. I wanted to skip and whistle but decided I'd better keep quiet. I didn't want to get arrested for disturbing the peace.

Chapter 6

PINK FLOCKED WALLPAPER. Lace around the pillow covers? Where was I? Awake but the images from my dream still lingered in my consciousness refusing to disappear as my mind sharpened. The body floating face down in an eddy.

I saw the femininity around me from the Flatville Bed and Breakfast, knew I was awake but couldn't stop the barrage of scenes coming in flashes. I was back standing on a bluff we'd called devil's jump. It was a twenty-foot overhang above the Green River. It was the right of passage into manhood. You were still a kid until you ran and jumped off the bluff into the river below.

My mind pulled me back and I didn't want to go. The soft pillow lulled me to sleep but my subconscious decided to relive the pain today. Damn. The opening day in the conference proved returning to Flatville a bad idea. Then Trudy in the bar and the Ram-and-Sam tag team. Nothing had changed from the summer between my freshman and sophomore year of high school—the best and worst of my life.

The images still flashed…the friendship, the adventure, the argument, and the drowning. I thought I had blocked the image of death but it rose to greet me. I could have saved Aaron with the lifesaving class my parents insisted I take, but I had run instead. The guilt pulled at my soul. I had to stop these images. I didn't want to remember. Damn Scott and Trudy for bringing it up last night.

Returning to sleep didn't work so I pulled to full wakefulness, wanting to see the lace and flowers, the here and now, but my ears pounded with the voices of fifteen-year-old kids locked in battle.

"You're chicken. Bawk, bawk." Ram imitated the clucking.

"Only sissies are afraid to jump." Sam added, dancing around the three of us. I remembered the cloud of dust he made. The pair dared us to jump in the river off the bluff's overhang.

Aaron had older brothers and was tougher than Scott and me. Scott had sisters but they were younger.

"At least we don't have to force people..." Aaron never completed the thought. Ram started toward him, eyes fierce and hard.

I saw the fear in Scott's and Aaron's faces, but Aaron stood tall. I'd taken ass-kicking from Ram before and wasn't anxious to do it again. Scott and I turned tail and ran and Sam was on our heels. "We'll make men out of you..."

Footsteps pounded behind me and I didn't know if it was friend or foe. I slowed and Scott caught up. We gasped for breath and listened but didn't hear anything and Aaron didn't appear on our heels.

We heard Sam's voice behind us. "At least Aaron wasn't afraid to jump. Bunch of cry babies. I'm going home. You sissies can cry to your mommas." He pushed past us continuing down the path. He turned for one final parting shot. "Babies."

"Are not," we'd said in unison. Sam gave us a disgusted look and moved out of sight away from the bluff.

Silently we debated what to do. Aaron hadn't joined us. Had he jumped? Was Ram punching his lights out? We reluctantly climbed back to the top of the overhang. It was empty. We looked around but could find no one. The only sound we heard was a car starting somewhere off in the distance.

Silently we turned back to the path we had escaped on only moments before.

The trail wound from the outcropping at a steep angle and made a sharp turn nearly to the river. Large trees and bushes grew along the side to stabilize the overhang. The path split with a twenty-foot leg that ended at the river. The other direction followed the river back to town.

We kept glancing from side to side expecting Aaron to pop out but not willing to meet each other's eyes or say anything. Aaron was good at hiding from the many times he hid from his brothers when he had ratted out their fun.

We were at the river's edge. Had Aaron jumped? I scanned the water for his lazy stroke pulling him to shore. I remembered the silence. No birds, no insects.

I looked back over my shoulder to the eddy under the bluff. Aaron was in the river. Not moving. We jumped in and pulled him out. I did everything I could. Breaths, pushing on his chest, repeating the procedure as the reality set in. We were too late.

With that image imprinted in my consciousness I became fully awake and the homey lace and flowers did nothing to eradicate the worst moment of my life. I needed coffee, black and an entire dozen doughnuts.

The sooner I inhaled my favorite comfort foods, the sooner the image would dim and then disappear. I hadn't had that nightmare for years and I didn't want it now. Thrusting myself up, I wanted to scream. My head felt like it was going to split in two. I wanted to find my pillow but knew the dream would rekindle. The pain was better than the memories.

As I shuffled to the bathroom, I allowed other images to come from happier times to dim the nightmare. The three Musketeers out exploring the wilderness along the Green River. It had been an afternoon of fun and frivolity that I had rarely seen under my parents' constant eye for education.

I could still remember the joy of the escape. It was nearing the end of summer vacation. Both mom and dad had meetings at the university where they taught. I had dutifully promised to read *War and Peace* while they were gone. It was to be the discussion at dinner that evening. I'd chucked the book and left right after they did and met Aaron and Scott at the Green River Park.

We'd left the park to explore along the river. We'd caught frogs and turtles and even a snake. We'd had sword fights with sticks and boasted about our prowess as pirates hiding loot in a secret spot.

As the hot water soothed my head, the happy memories and dreams drifted back to history. The present flooded in and part of me wished for the past. It was Saturday and I didn't have anything to do today but work on getting my award-winning story. Every time I thought about it I wanted to slap my forehead. Stupid, stupid, stupid.

I felt off from my dream and a bit of a hangover made my thoughts cobwebby and slow. I looked forward to the breakfast portion of my stay and hoped for bacon and eggs and all the trimmings. I didn't expect doughnuts but homemade pastries might fit the bill.

The couple who ran the place were in their sixties and chatty, especially Harold who was on his second marriage with Katherine. Harold had lived next door to me on the corner lot when I was growing up. It was a shock to see how much he had aged. I thought he was old when I was a teen.

He'd been a plumber and had fixed the toilet for us a couple of times when my toys accidentally fell in. My parents frowned on socializing with anyone who didn't have an advanced degree. I remembered his first wife fondly although I couldn't remember her name. She'd never gone to college but would give me cookies when I was out riding my bike if I stopped on the other street and used their house as a shield from my parents' watchful eyes. Timothy and Erin Malone didn't approve of sweets or anything that wasn't organic or whole wheat well before organic ever described high-grade vegetables and fruit.

I ran through possible reasons to leave right after I ate so as not to have to stay and chat about me. I opened my door and heard a commotion from below. I reached the edge of the balustrade and looked down into the front foyer from the white railing.

Harold was talking to two policemen and blocking their path.

"I will not have you clambering the stairs disturbing all my guests. You wait here and I will get Mr. Malone. He has not risen yet."

I stepped back and tried to determine what was happening. My late night, lack of sleep, unsettling dreams and a bit too much beer delayed my quick analysis. My first instinct was to run and had served me well in the past. Then I remembered I'd run and Aaron had died. Damn memories!

"Why don't you gentleman step into the dining room and have yourselves a cup of Mrs. Shoemaker's coffee? It's better than what you get at Seven-Eleven."

Harold waited for the officers to leave and then one leg at a time climbed the stairs in my direction. No hustle or bustle in his demeanor.

As my brain kicked in I wondered why the police were looking for me. In Grand River, I worked closely with the boys in blue and wouldn't dread their call. In Flatville their presence was a vise on my stomach, bile rising or was that the hangover. Why were they here? They certainly weren't going to help me get my exclusive so I could blow this town. If I had to guess this would be Sam Jones throwing his weight around like he did as a kid, just because he could. I took it in my teens but I would be damned if I was going to take it as an adult. I was not going to run.

"Ahh. There you are, Mr. Malone. Two police officers are in the dining room and would like to talk to you."

"Any idea what they want?" I looked directly at Harold and saw the intelligence behind his eyes that I never noticed growing up.

"Can't say for sure but scuttlebutt around town is that a woman's body was found." His eyes turned hard and gave me the once over. "You got in kind of late, Mr. Malone."

Great. Now I had a curfew. Why can't they have real hotels where you can come and go as you please and no one knows.

"I didn't have anything to do with it." I returned his stare, my agitation rising.

"Didn't say you did."

I suddenly realized the old man was a foxy one. He'd remarked last night that I was the only guest. He was giving me time to pull myself together.

"What should I do?" I wanted his take on the situation. He'd lived in this town for sixty years and knew the local law enforcement as well as a good share of gossip.

"I wouldn't let them back you in a corner and I wouldn't let them get you alone in a room. Bad things happen when people go in for questioning."

My reporter sense went off. This could get me out of my jam with the cub reporters. Police brutality, beating confessions out of people. It made me almost giddy to be their suspect. Sanity set in. I couldn't write about what happened to me. I needed to find others. Mitch Malone was on another hot story and the *Flatville Gazette* staff would have a first-hand look of how a real reporter got the scoop. That is if I could stay out of the slammer. I knew Sam wouldn't hesitate to toss me in and throw away the key.

Then I thought about the body that had been found. They couldn't possibly think I had anything to do with it. I only just arrived in town. Then I thought of Biff and Bob. Sure I wasn't happy with them, but could they have tried my techniques and gotten into trouble they couldn't get out of? A new layer of guilt crashed down. Was I doomed to always cause death when in Flatville?

"Any suggestions?"

"You need an attorney." He nodded his head confirming his own statement.

"Who? It would take hours to get one from Grand River who could fight for my release on the first amendment, freedom of speech."

"I have just the man. Let me make a call and see if he can pop by. Why don't you give those cops about fifteen minutes to enjoy their coffee and sweets the misses has prepared before making your appearance? I'll tell them you're in the shower."

My mouth drooled at the mention of sweets and hoped the officers wouldn't eat them all. I was betting Harold was as sharp as he appeared and I had a feeling this was one bet I didn't want to lose.

I returned to my room and sat on the bed looking at the clock. Eight fifteen. I needed to fill the time and pulled out two fresh notebooks from the twenty-pack in my suitcase. You could never carry too many notebooks. I started making notes of what I needed to do. I had to find people who had been arrested and interrogated. I needed to find several to develop a pattern of behavior and have at least three maybe more willing to talk on the record. Three would be needed because chances were they were convicted of a crime and would need more collaboration.

Chapter 7

I HEARD VOICES again but couldn't make out what they were saying through my closed door. Then the doorbell chimed.

I heard Harold's heavy tread on the steps and met him at my door. He waved me down the stairs.

"Mr. Malone, two police officers are here to see you and your nine o'clock appointment with Clive Darrow has arrived."

I didn't have any appointments so I figured Clive was my attorney. His name was familiar but I couldn't place it.

I nodded to Harold and followed him into an old-style parlor stuffed with coordinating furniture. I had a choice of two loveseats, one in flowers the other in coordinating stripes and a solid, maroon-colored pincushion chair. The cops were on the striped seat and a lanky, latte-colored man with tight-cropped, black, curly hair sat on the opposite side. I shook his hand assuming he was Darrow and then faced the officers.

"You wanted to see me?" I tried to look friendly and helpful. The officers looked anything but. Annoyance oozed from waiting although tea cups were empty on the table in front of them as was a plate of something sweet I could only discern from the crumbs that were left. My stomach rumbled.

Harold shuffled in and took the only empty chair.

"Mr. Malone. I'm Officer Sweeney and this is Officer Jacobson." He nodded to his fellow brother in blue. "We'd like to ask you a few questions. Where were you last night?" This from the larger of the two cops who looked uncomfortable on the spindly-legged furniture.

"The Main Street Pub for dinner."

"What time did you leave?" This from the other cop, Jacobson.

"I'm not sure. What is all this about?" I wanted to pull out my notebook but realized that might not be a good move.

"The time?" The first cop nudged.

If they weren't going to answer my questions, I wasn't going to answer theirs.

"Hmmm." I brought my finger to my chin. "Am I a suspect in something?"

"Why would you think so?" This again from the big cop.

"You're here at the crack of dawn to ask me questions and you won't tell me what it is about. I'm concerned."

"Nothing to concern yourself with, Mr. Malone. Just answer the questions." The little guy, Jacobson, spoke up, a fake smile trying to put me at ease. He was lying. I would bet my next exclusive on it.

I saw a small smile play across Mr. Darrow's face.

"At the bar last night I had a," I paused for a minute trying to figure out how best to word the altercation. "Err, discussion with your police chief. I didn't walk away with a feeling that he was concerned with justice. Hence my hesitancy to answer any questions. Am I being charged with a crime?"

"Not at this time." Jacobson said. Another fake smile, more of a leer. "We just want some information about the whereabouts of people last night."

"I see. I might be able to answer more if I know what this relates to."

My attorney coughed into his hand and I thought he might have been laughing.

"We are not at liberty to say the exact nature of our inquiry." The big guy ground this out between clenched teeth.

I was tired of this cat and mouse game. I wanted to force them into some type of action. "Then I apologize but I have other matters to attend to. If you will excuse me..." I let the words hang there as I started to rise. Both men opposite rose as if on cue. Harold swung his head from side to side as if he had been volleying words.

"Mr. Malone. You are under arrest for the murder of Trudy Harrison." The big guy reached for his belt and pulled out a pair of handcuffs.

I couldn't move. Trudy was dead? I had had breakfast with her less than twelve hours ago. How? Why? I felt the blood seep from my face.

"Excuse me, gentlemen." Mr. Darrow rose to his feet. "May I see the warrant?"

The big man's face went red.

"You do have a warrant?" Mr. Darrow stepped between the cop and me.

My attorney looked up but indignation was oozing out of every pore and the larger man started to shrink into his newly-shined boots.

His partner stepped forward. "We don't need a warrant." He pulled his handcuffs out from his belt, the metal clanking together like the door of a cell slamming shut.

I gulped, not a practical joke. These cops actually thought I'd murdered Trudy.

"I don't think so, gentlemen. You have asked to speak to my client and he has inquired about the nature of the charges and if he was a suspect. You can't lie to entrap him and then arrest him."

I wanted to cheer Mr. Darrow. He knew how to put cops back on their heels.

"Please outline under what probable cause you have to make an arrest. It simply can't be because my client refuses to answer any questions. When you have that warrant or probable cause, please call my office. I will accompany Mr. Malone when he turns himself in. Good day gentleman."

I was immobilized by the quick turn of events until Mr. Darrow grabbed my arm and propelled me into the formal dining room where a buffet-style breakfast sat on some type of glorified dresser along one wall. A table with chairs for twelve held place settings of fine china for four.

"Shall we eat?" Mr. Darrow grabbed a plate off the table and began serving himself. "Bluffing officers makes me hungry."

I glanced back to see the door closing on the men in blue. I quickly grabbed a plate and followed Darrow's lead.

"That was a nasty bit of business," Harold said returning. "I bolted the front door and hopefully we won't be having any interruptions."

As I scooped scrambled eggs onto my plate and two slices of some kind of coffeecake, I heard another door close and wondered if both slices would fit in my mouth before I was hauled off to jail.

Instead of boys in blue, Harold's wife, Kate, entered through the swinging door that I assumed was a kitchen. "The town is abuzz with this murder business. People are scared." She wrung her hands on a dish towel.

Harold went to her and guided her to a seat at the table. He got her a teabag located near the coffeecake and retrieved a carafe filling the delicate china cup with the steaming liquid.

"Was that a police car leaving as I walked up?" She pulled the teabag from its wrapper and dunked it into the hot water.

"Yes, dear, but have some tea and let's let the gentlemen eat their breakfast and then we can sort this all out."

I settled myself and my plate at the table and started in on the coffeecake. It melted in my mouth and I forgot about the cops and murder. I may have to rethink my doughnut diet.

"Mrs. Shoemaker, this coffeecake is delicious. Did you make it?"

"Yes, I did. Thank you, dear." She smoothed an errant piece of hair behind her ear, beaming as she looked around the table. "You can call me Kate." She batted an eyelash in my direction. Was she flirting with me? I looked at her husband.

Mr. Shoemaker beamed back at his wife and then nodded in my direction.

I smiled at the pair and then dug into the eggs and made short work of them.

"Mitch Malone, I would like to formally introduce you to Clive Darrow. A new edition to Flatville but he has developed an excellent reputation for helping his clients."

I hurriedly wiped my mouth with a real cloth napkin and then reached over the table holding out my hand. "Pleased to meet you and thank you."

The attorney took it and smiled. "My pleasure. Any time I can thwart the department's high-handed tactics and preserve the Constitution, it's a good day."

"Do the police often abuse their office?" The reporter in me was reaching back for my notebook. I set it on the table and pulled the pen from its spine. I caught sight of the pastry platter on the counter behind Clive and wondered if I could refill my plate.

As if Harold had read my mind he walked to the sideboard, lifted the platter and returned to the table, offering seconds to Clive first and then myself. I added two more pieces to my now empty plate.

"I remember you had a sweet tooth, Mitch." Harold returned the plate with the other food.

I recalled the cookies Harold's first wife used to have sitting at the table in their back yard. My parents didn't believe sugar was good for a growing boy and an applesauce/wheat germ combination was used in its place. Nothing fluffy or tasty about my mother's baking.

The first Mrs. Shoemaker could make a fine cookie. I would sneak through the thick hedge surrounding my backyard throwing a ball out in front of me. I never played with the ball but whenever I rolled it through the hedge, I was offered a cookie from her never-empty tray on the table and then a glass of Kool-aid. The combination is still one of my favorites.

"Mr. Malone." Darrow wiped his mouth and set his napkin on his plate.

"Please call me Mitch," I said trying not to eject coffee cake crumbs across the table as I spoke.

"Mitch, those officers will be returning and they will be taking you into custody. If there is one thing I've learned is once they have their teeth into someone, nothing can change their mind." Clive pushed his plate toward the center of the table.

"What is going on and why am I a suspect? They can't possibly have any evidence."

"Trudy was such a sweet girl." Mrs. Shoemaker said raising her cup to her lips.

"Seems she was found out on the Green River bluff by some hikers early this morning. Rumor has it she was beaten, raped and then murdered." Harold outlined what he knew.

"Oh, this is just awful." Mrs. Shoemaker's cup clattered into its saucer. Harold grabbed her hand and squeezed.

"They think I did this?" I remembered last night. Trudy out of hand and drunk. What had she done after I dropped her at her parent's house? My prints must have been all over her car. I'd left it parked on the street and walked the couple of blocks to the B & B. My car still was parked at the bar.

Guilt must have suffused my features.

"You want to tell me what happened?" Clive's voice was soft, almost hypnotic compared to the hard edge when he talked to the cops.

This was bad. I wouldn't be getting an exclusive anytime soon. I would be Biff and Bob's exclusive in a town they claimed never had anything worthwhile happen.

Chapter 8

I LOOKED AT the Shoemakers and wondered if they could be forced to repeat what I said to my attorney. I thought Mr. Shoemaker could be a cagey guy but the missus might like to gossip a bit too much.

As if reading my mind, Mr. Shoemaker rose and held the chair for his second wife. "Why don't we just take care of this food while these gentlemen talk?" I thought Kate might have looked a bit crestfallen but she followed her husband.

The first thing off the sideboard was the coffeecake followed by the scrambled eggs. I wanted to tell them the food could stay, but they had to go. The couple returned and Harold filled my cup with hot coffee then they disappeared with more breakfast debris.

"Want to tell me what happened last night?" Clive's voice mesmerized me. He would be good at convincing a jury but I hoped it wouldn't get to that.

How to begin. I'd never been much good at telling my own story but best to give Clive as much to work with as I could. It began when I first returned to Flatville—the worst mistake of my life.

"It started when my first session at the newspaper went into the toilet. I lost my temper with some smart-ass, green reporters. I went to the Main Street Pub to unwind and grab something to eat. What I didn't know was that my class reunion was going on in a back room and eventually spilled out into the bar area."

"Keep going," Clive encouraged nodding in my direction.

I related the confrontation with Ram, Sam's appearance and comments.

"I left the bar and saw Trudy crying and trying to get into her car. She was in no shape to drive. Not sure about me either but I could unlock a car door. I helped her in and even fastened her seatbelt for her. We drove and got some breakfast in River Crossing, the only place I knew had a twenty-four-hour diner, turns out the McDonalds there keeps late hours as well. After that, I took her to her parents' place. She went inside, I walked the eight blocks back here. My car is still at the pub."

"I see." Clive's noncommittal reply worried me.

"Wait. I remember something else. Her brother, Kim, waited for her at the house. He wanted money and she refused. He was pretty upset. Maybe he came back?"

Harold entered the room and started clearing more off the table. "What I want to know is how she got from her parents' place to the bluff. Someone would have had to see her," Harold said as he grabbed the salt and pepper and retreated back through the swinging door.

I looked at Clive and we both smiled. He'd been listening at the door.

"Why would she have left the house? It had to be someone she knew?" Clive mused aloud.

"My prints in the car make me an easy target. If Chief Sam Jones is anything like he was in high school, he would love to railroad a successful, big-city reporter into jail just because he could." I took a drink of the coffee willing my brain to think faster. It wouldn't be long and those red-neck cops would be back with a warrant. Clive and his fancy lawyering wouldn't stop Sam from putting my carcass in jail.

Harold swung through the door and grabbed the butter and a couple pieces of errant silverware. "Why would anyone take her to that bluff and why would she go?" The words muttered as if to himself but loud enough for us to hear.

I rose from the table. "I can't sit here and wait for them to come back and they will. I need to investigate just like it was an exclusive story."

"Good plan, boy." Harold nodded his head in agreement.

"Now don't go getting in the way but anything you find will only help your case. I agree the police aren't going to look hard for other suspects when you are easy pickings. I'll nose around the courthouse and see what I can find and what the grapevine says." Clive started to rise.

"That would be great." I held out my hand to Clive. He seemed to be a great person to have in your corner, I had to trust my instincts on that.

"Kate and I will check with neighbors and such and see what rumors are floating. How about we met back here around five-thirty? Kate mentioned some fried chicken and mashed potatoes for dinner. Consider this your formal invitation to join us. She doesn't know how to cook for just two."

"That sounds delicious." My stomach rumbled in anticipation.

"Thank you, Mr. and Mrs. Shoemaker. I would be delighted to join you."

"Kate and Harold, Clive. We don't stand on formalities." Harold exited through the kitchen door.

Clive and I looked at each other and as with one mind, we headed for the door.

It was Saturday. I instinctively headed for the newspaper office, not sure it would be open over the weekend. The next edition didn't come out until Monday. The Grand River Sunday paper was delivered and the local *Gazette* only published Monday through Saturday.

As I walked, I tried to develop a plan. I glanced around looking for police cars but also noticed the old-style architecture. Large homes sported varying colors and styles from Victorian to traditional saltbox to early American. The yards manicured by high school boys, the only ones capable of withstanding the heat to earn enough to take their sweetheart out for ice cream later. When mentioning small town America, these streets typified a slower, quieter pace, except for Trudy.

After the grand homes, I reached the business district which consisted of the city square – a park complete with gazebo and grandstand. Across the street retail shops surrounded it on three sides and the county building and courthouse dominating the final side.

I crossed the square and went another block past it to the newspaper. The dark front signaled what I knew. Closed. However, someone may be working on something. I walked down the parking lot along the side of the building to the employee entrance. Locked. So much for my first seminar convincing them to work harder. Another solid steel door looked little used next to a larger rollup door in metal building at a right angle to the brick building housing a line of window for the newsroom and publishers office. Might as well try them all, I didn't have a plan B.

The door opened in my hand, but it was dark inside except for large looming shadows. I thought fleetingly of a haunted house in a B-movie where the audience always knows the hero shouldn't go in.

Before the door closed I saw a room with counters around the walls and then the door clicked shut and all was black.

"Hello." My voice cracked and while blind, the dark provided relief from the heat the same way a basement does. I hoped my eyes would adjust before I tripped over something.

"Back here," came a voice over to my left.

I wasn't sure what area of the paper I was in. Suddenly the lights flooded on and I brought my hand up to shield my eyes from the fluorescent glare.

I crossed through the outer room into what looked to be an old print area complete with a small web press that didn't compare to the three-story monster at the *Journal*. The web press was so called because the six-foot rolls of newsprint were snaked through the many rollers containing the tin prints of the pages. When the paper came out the end through the web of machinery, every page was in order, the sections together ready for delivery.

"Can I help you?"

I turned and identified the voice of a short, dark-haired girl wearing a black plastic apron and blending in nicely with the printing press. Either grease or ink covered various appendages including her cute, pug nose.

"I'm Mitch Malone. I'm here…" Before I could get the rest of the reason why I was here, she made short work of the distance and pumped my hand.

"Pleased to meet you. I love your stuff. I want to be a big-time reporter. I plan to attend Central Michigan University the following fall. Wanted to sit in on your seminars but we had press problems." She motioned back toward the machine with a crescent wrench in her hand.

Black covered my hand where the first eager beaver I'd encountered had left her mark.

Her unexpected enthusiasm stopped me as did the marker on my hand. Someone at this rag actually liked my stuff. I wouldn't mind teaching her some of the finer points of investigative journalism. She was eager to learn.

"Thank you. Are you the only one here?"

"Yeah. The part finally came for the repair. We only use this old girl for local printing jobs but it helps to keep the bottom line in the black or so my dad says. He's the publisher." She patted the press as if she was an old friend.

My face must have fallen.

"Whatcha need? There ain't anything I can't find here. Been helping out after school since fifth grade."

What did I need help with? Maybe not everyone in Flatville was a moron like the two in the news room. "Know anything about the body they found this morning?"

"They found a body, golly gee, no. Can we go to the crime scene?" Enthusiasm poured from her voice as her body started toward the door pulling off the apron as she went.

I wanted to pull her back by the long braid that hung down her back. I couldn't use a kid, too green. "Sorry. I just needed some help with research."

The light died in her eyes replaced with a flash of determination. "I get it. I'm too young. I can strip apart this old press and put it back with my eyes closed but I'm not good enough to work with the great and mighty Mitch Malone."

I opened my mouth to console her but realized I didn't even know her name. I shut it.

"No worries, man. I get it all the time. From my dad, from those arrogant reporters in the newsroom. I'll show you all. You just wait. I'm going to get a Pulitzer." She put the apron on a peg by a door.

The look of resolve in her eye left no doubt she would get the highest award for journalism and I shared her opinion of the newsroom. I'd better watch my back or keep this spitfire in front of me. Maybe she could be of use.

"Now that's showing how green you are." Her eyes flared at my use of green but I knew she wouldn't take any patronizing from me. "You want to go off all half cocked wanting to see your first dead body. The body isn't going to tell you anything you can print in the paper. You need sources for that."

I saw her nod and knew I had her hooked. She would be a great little research assistant. "Now to get the most of your sources, you have to research. Know what questions to ask. That's why I came here before going to look at the crime scene. Let's see what we can find out about the victim and then we'll know where to look and who to ask that knew her well."

"Gee, Mr. Malone. I could learn a lot from you." All traces of anger and hurt were gone.

"Thanks…" I let the words hang out there waiting for her to drop in her name.

"Scoop Bradshaw." She stuck out her hand and I shook it again adding more darkness to my hand. She caught me staring at it. "Sorry about that." She reached into her back pocket and pulled out a red rag that only had a few spots on it. I was able to wipe off most of the black residue.

"Thanks. Seriously, your parents named you Scoop?" I returned the rag and she started cleaning her hands.

"No. My real name is Sarah." She said it with a nasal inflection. "My mom came from money and I'm named after her grandmother who she hoped would leave her a pile of money in her will. So I'm stuck with Sarah Elizabeth Montgomery Bradshaw."

"And Scoop? Was that because you always wanted to be a reporter?"

"No. Daddy says I was visiting him at the paper when I was only a toddler and they were having awful problems with the press run. That's when the whole paper was printed here. The paper kept ripping and they couldn't figure out why. I toddled over and pulled out a screw that was caught between the printing cylinders. Daddy said I just scooped it out and the name stuck. Problem is I've been working on this old press ever since and I want to get my name on top of the news story, not the grease monkey behind the scenes."

She took in a big gulp of breath and let it out slowly. "Sorry. Daddy says when I get excited, there is just no shutting me up."

I nodded but knew I needed to get to business. I didn't know when the cops would be back and this time my attorney wouldn't intimidate them.

"Do you have a morgue?"

"Sure, in the basement of the hospital. We're going to go look at the dead body there?" She was clearly mystified and it took me a minute to figure out the misunderstanding.

"No. At the *Grand River Journal* we call our library, where we keep all the back editions, the morgue. I don't know why." I shrugged my shoulders.

"Why didn't you say so? It's back here." She walked around the giant press and to a solid closed door with no markings. She opened and walked in to the dark interior.

I was following but nervous about stumbling in the dark or worse yet landing on the teen or grabbing her to break my fall. "Is there a light?"

"Oh, sorry. I'm so used to taking this route, I don't bother with the light. There is a hallway that runs up that way." She pointed toward the front in the opposite direction. "I usually have grease stains and don't need to be the butt of any more jokes in the newsrooms. This gets me to the front without having to go near the newsroom."

This was good information. I would want to avoid Biff and Bob. Scoop opened a door and we entered a room no bigger than a conference room. Narrow windows lined the ceiling along one side letting in plenty of light. Every wall spot that wasn't a doorway was a four-drawer file cabinet in an array of nondescript colors.

"I know this room ain't pretty, but Thelma doesn't let anyone touch it. She prides herself on finding anything."

I knew the loveable dragon who kept the *Grand River Journal* morgue and understood the need to keep others out or no one would find anything.

"Can we search?"

"Oh yeah." She had an impish grin. "I know her system. What are we looking for?"

"Trudy Harrison."

Scoop moved some papers around a desk in the center of the room and to my surprise there was a computer and some type of printer. "Thelma spends her days scanning the old stories and cataloguing them electronically.

She tapped the keys and the screen fired up. More tapping. Trudy came up looking gorgeous and just as I remembered her. The colored shot showed Trudy in a red dress with a white sash and tiara. The beauty had her beast, Ram with black lines under his eyes and the football pads extending his already bulky frame.

Scoop started to tap more keys but I touched her hand and moved in

50   W.S. Gager

closer to the screen. "Can you blow this up?"

"Sure, what part?"

I pointed to her face. As the photo enlarged, I could see that Trudy's smile resembled more of a grimace. I hit the down arrow and the photo moved from the faces to the midsection.

Ram's hand wrapped around Trudy's wrist like a vise causing a little blurring of the picture from the movement. Even back then, Trudy wasn't as enamored of Ram as I had thought. What else had I missed?

I signaled Scoop to move on. Trudy's yearbook photo in a graduation section, one of her working on decorating for prom also filled the screen. Nothing amiss in any of those. She tapped more keys but nothing more appeared.

I rubbed the back of my neck. What was I missing? Hadn't Trudy gone off to college? Did she never leave? Never married? Wait she told me she was divorced. No mention of the nuptials or the split. She must have lived out of town then. Some of the cobwebs were clearing from my brain and I remembered snatches of her comments that made no sense at the time.

"Okay, Mr. Malone. What else do we need to search for?"

Startled out of my memories, I wanted more information. "Search Richard A. Malone, Jr." The screen filled with dozens of references and continued on for two more. We paged through them and saw the homecoming shot again, grad photo, scholarship mention, dean's list announcements for four years at Michigan State where he was only the back-up quarterback and never took a snap. The next shot was Ram and his dad, Rich Sr. in front of Malone Hardware, going into the family business. One was a carbon copy of the other. I heard an impatient puff from over my shoulder. I couldn't discern the look in her eye.

"You got something to say?"

"Yeah. My dad lets that guy roll all over him. Always giving him free advertising for mistakes in the paper that aren't his fault. It's like he does it on purpose."

I nodded. It sounded exactly like Ram. Always trying to muscle something out of someone.

"Oops." Scoop put her hand over her mouth. "Sorry."

"For what?"

"I didn't mean to insult your relative. I shouldn't have said anything. Daddy's always getting on me about being tactful. I think it and it just blurts right out of my mouth."

"No offense taken. I don't care for him myself."

I return to the listing but found nothing else of note but small mentions for joining the Rotary or Chamber of Commerce, taking office and leaving with a trinket for all his hard work and quotes extolling the work he was responsible for. A textbook pillar of the community. Not the control freak and bully I knew.

Scoop was getting impatient for action. Couldn't blame her but I had one more name to search. Samuel Jones. His history eerily followed Ram. Wide Receiver at State who actually got game time. Degree, criminal justice, joining the sheriff's department as a deputy and then applying for the city chief of police position when Ram was on the city council. No favoritism there. The rest was clips of him arresting bad guys on a regular basis. Who knew Flatville had such a high crime rate and now murder? Time to look into the crime I was accused of. Time for Mitch Malone to beat out other reporters and even police for the story. This wasn't how I wanted to get the exclusive but when facing a murder charge, you have to go where the news takes you.

"Now we go to the murder scene."

Scoop jumped back from the keyboard and hit the keys to shut the computer down. Her excitement was contagious as I remembered my first murder story. That was a long time ago and this one was hitting closer to home and I felt more desperation and sadness than thrill. This one was personal, not because I was top on the suspect's list but Trudy was a friend. For that reason alone I would find the true murderer.

It was time to get to the bottom of who killed Trudy Harrison.

CHAPTER 9

MY SLEUTHING COMPANION was a motor mouth.

"What are we going to see? Will the body still be there? Are we going to jump the police tape?" The questions just kept coming. It was like a radio in the background. You needed it on, but you tuned it out.

Scoop was driving her little car. Seem prudent to take hers because I didn't want to walk the couple blocks in the sun that had risen high and hot on the mid July morning.

Getting to the bluff was easy on foot, just five minutes from downtown. Driving there took about fifteen minutes because of the river's meandering path and the lack of bridges crossing it. I wasn't in a hurry to get there.

I had bigger worries and a ghost to face. I hadn't been to the bluff since the day my childhood friend, Aaron, died. Time was standing still as I replayed that day over and over. The drive seemed like hours as I was caught in the revolving nightmare of my youth. One I had successfully forgotten until being sent here for the damn workshop. I knew coming to Flatville would be bad but I had no idea how bad.

"How we going to handle this, Mr. Malone?" We were in an older model black Volkswagen with our shoulders nearly touching.

We drove past the river which glinted in the sunlight and rippled as the water's carefree path on its way to join another river on its way to Lake Michigan. I tried to concentrate on the route it would take, emptying from here to the Grand River and then to the big lake and freedom. I was stuck watching the sun glint off the Green River for the next several days when I wanted to be back in the city watching the Grand River. I tried to think of anything but what I faced. If Ram and Sam took control, the only water I would watch would be in a metal sink in a cell.

"Can I ask the questions?"

My heart hammered. I held my breath. I heard Scoop but had no idea what she was saying. I gulped air trying to fill my lungs but it never eased the tightness in my chest. The closer we got, the more I felt out of control.

"You okay, Mr. Malone?" My passenger stopped mid-diatribe and stared at me in concern.

"Just fine." The words whistled through my clenched teeth. She pulled into a grassy flat spot that was smooth compared to the road we had just travelled. The bluff was all public lands nestled on an edge of the National Forest. The road barely a two-track.

Sweat beaded on my forehead. My hands were clammy. I was fourteen again. Remembering what I had tried so hard to forget. Trees reaching to the sky, ferns covering the ground. The sounds of leaves rustling in the wind, birds singing. I tried to will myself back to the present. Instead I was running like the coward I was.

Scoop touched my arm, alarm on her face.

"No one's here." I heard the disappointment in her voice and grabbed on to it pulling myself to the present.

"Interesting," was all I could get out but I felt the panic recede. I looked around noticing the parking lot and its lack of occupants beside us. I double checked my surroundings to make sure in my stupor we'd gone to the right place.

I exited the car and took a deep breath filling my lungs and slowing my heart. I could do this, I told myself.

I'd never driven to the river before. We meandered here through the city park to the national forest when none of my compatriots had a driver's license. After, it didn't matter. Aaron, Scott and I frolicked at being cowboys and Indians, cops and robbers, explorers and wild bears. You name it; our imaginations dreamed it.

Then it ended. Now I was headed to the bluff, the place that contained the worst nightmares of my life including last night's. Why had I come back? Why did I need to see where Trudy died? I needed to focus on Trudy, not Aaron.

We walked in silence toward the path to the bluff. I was glad for the quiet but it left me with my thoughts. Had Scoop realized something was wrong? Nothing I could do about it now. I just needed to focus on the task at hand. Forget the past. Push it back to the black recesses of my mind where it had been banished.

From the parking lot, a well worn path ascended three-hundred yards at a steep incline filled with thirty-year-old oaks, pines and aspens to reach the bluff. Within twenty feet the forest swallowed us and any sounds from human interlopers.

We had only entered the darkened, tree-covered area and could see the sunshine from the clearing by the river ahead. Odd, no yellow crime-scene tape barred our entrance. An ordinary picnic spot, no cop blocked our path, nothing.

I surmised that maybe they had finished. If a hiker had found her, that would give the cops six or eight hours or more to gather the makings of their case. My compatriot rushed on ahead. What would we find when we entered the open area? Or closer to the river? I remembered it as an old campsite with a clearing, that hadn't changed. Beyond, the ground dropped twenty-feet from centuries of river erosion. The rite of passage of my youth. You weren't a man unless you ran and jumped into the river below. Aaron had been more of a man than both Scott and I and he never reached manhood.

Stop thinking about the past. Look at the here and now. I commanded myself to the task at hand before I was hauled off to jail. I settled somewhat. Clear in my direction. Comforted by my need to be a reporter at a crime scene.

I wished I had grabbed some coffee cake to go at the bed and breakfast but I would have to do this on my now hungry stomach. Nearly four hours had passed since the cops came to call.

We stood at the edge of the clearing surveying it. I could feel Scoop's excitement to run into the fray, but I held out my arm forcing her to stop. The clearing looked much as I had remembered it. Too much so. How could this be a crime scene? Foot prints were visible everywhere in the dirt that was part sand and part ashes. Years of campfires made it silt that would only hold an impression for a short period of time. Lots of people had been here recently, that was obvious. What wasn't obvious was any sense of a crime scene.

I stepped forward and concentrated on what I saw or rather didn't see. For once Scoop was silent and not pulling at the reins to explore. She sensed something was wrong, but too inexperienced to know what.

With each step forward I checked the prints, all boot marks. I looked at Scoop's feet and saw running shoes stained with black ink. I looked behind her and saw the wavy-lined tread. I didn't see the print from the high heels adorning Trudy's slim feet. Those marks would have been easy to spot, inverted funnels in a zigzagged path. Had Flatville's blundering officers obliterated every print?

Or was Trudy dumped here like a rag doll and barely made an impression? Trudy had been all flash and energy and to be anything else was wrong. My anger rose at the thought. Anger pushed the darkness of memories back.

The boot marks intensified just before the rock-circled fire pit. We approached cautiously. Nothing of value was visible in the dirt.

"Is this really the crime scene?" Scoop's voice awed.

"Yes and no. They say her body was found here but she wasn't killed here." My voice was flat.

"How can you tell?" Energy infused her voice.

"No footprints. Trudy was wearing three-inch white stiletto heels last night with a white skirt. Any footprints would have been labeled and not stepped on. They're not here."

"Could she have been barefoot? Those heels are hard to walk on in this sandy stuff."

I hadn't thought about that. Maybe my motor mouth companion might have her uses.

"Good deduction, Watson. However, nothing even looks like it was tagged and photographed."

"What would that look like, Sherlock?" She stifled a laugh as she said the great detective's name.

My pupil was eager to learn and I felt too tired to teach, but did the best I could.

"There would be two lines about an inch and a half long and about an inch and a half apart. It would be a tent-shaped number correlating to a sketch made at the scene marking where it was found. The photo would show what the evidence was before it was bagged."

I started walking back to the path and the car when voices carried.

I wanted to hide and scanned the area. It was a visceral reaction from long ago. Scoop looked down the path.

"Who do you suppose that is? Someone trying to steal our story?" Her voice was tough; she could be a thug if she wanted.

I shook my head. "Probably gawkers wanting a thrill. Let's get out of here."

We headed down the path. On impulse I turned and pulled my small camera from my jacket pocket. Just before we hit the path, I took a photo of the scene and then a close-up shot of where I believed the body had been found by the configuration of foot prints. I also took photos of the clearest foot prints but figured the inexperienced cops at their first major crime scene didn't know any better.

I looked across the end of the bluff and to the river and far bank beyond. Shivering, I turned and walked back the way we had come. I will not remember. I will not remember. I just kept mentally repeating that phrase. With each step the darkness receded further.

We passed a group of teenagers that Scoop nodded toward as we walked around each other. She didn't talk to them. We just kept going.

As we got to the car my curiosity won out over thinking about death. I didn't want to talk about the murder and lodged on to the only topic I could think of. "Did you know those kids?"

"They go to my school." Her tone, sullen, confrontational.

"Do you not like them?"

Scoop shrugged her shoulders. "I don't have much time to socialize. I've got work at the paper and I'm going to be a big time reporter just like you." Her tone brightened at the end.

Her statement bothered me. She was young, pretty if you discounted the ink. She should have a boyfriend. In a flash realization hit me. She was hiding from something too.

Chapter 10

"SO TELL ME about the reporters at the *Gazette*." I wasn't one of those we-need-to-break-the-silence kind of guys but I wanted information.

As we drove back to the newspaper I banished my demons at least temporarily. I needed to get some of the politics figured out at the newspaper and in the community. I might as well start with Scoop. Maybe something might slip about her own situation. I had the impression she didn't have any friends her own age. I hoped she had someone at the newspaper. It didn't sound like she got along with her dad, the publisher, or any reporters.

"Jerks."

I felt the same way but I needed to find out why. "I figured that." I gave a little self-depreciating laugh.

"Biff and Bob treat me like I don't know anything. They've been here less than a year and just out of college, but they don't know anything. I tried to tell them who to talk to when they first got here but they couldn't be bothered."

She left a lot out but I'm sure their rebuke was demeaning and never ended. Similar to my own experience.

"What about the others?"

"Mary, the features editor, is okay but she won't do anything out of her way to help. She does her job. That's it. Chuck, the editor, is an older version of Biff and Bob. He's been here a few years and knows not to mess with me but he'll be gone in a year or less. Onto bigger seas. He's hoping to follow you to the *Grand River Journal*. He hasn't kissed up yet?"

I shook my head and braced myself as she negotiated a turn a little faster than necessary.

"He will."

"What about your dad?"

"He's the publisher. He hates it that I am so good with the press. He forbade me after I entered high school. Said he could handle it and I should concentrate on having fun. The iron monster broke. Old Louie is okay but only knows the basics. Dad hated it when he had to ask me. Had to go to the school and pull me out so the paper would get out. He wanted to die." She rolled her eyes.

I glanced at her as she pulled to a stop sign. She sat straighter now, a funny smirk played at the corner of her mouth.

"Are you as good with all machines or just the presses?"

"Not sure. I've never been able to work on any other machines besides the press. My dad wouldn't hear of it."

"So you want to be a reporter?"

"More than anything. I've taken all the English classes I can at my school. I've applied to Central Michigan for the following year. That's where my mom went, then to University of Michigan for her master's where she met my dad. She was a reporter too."

We'd pulled into the paper and Scoop shut off the engine. I waited for her to volunteer. Kids like Scoop wouldn't take well to questioning. They had to get to it in their own time. I would wait. Why I wanted to, mystified me. Other people's feelings never seemed important but something in what Scoop didn't say called to me. Reminded me of a kid forced to read books when he wanted to run outside and play baseball.

"My mom died." The voice soft, almost a whisper.

My gut said she'd never told anyone before. Everyone in this town would know every tragedy and triumph. That was the curse of Flatville. Everyone knew everyone else's business. I waited.

"She and my dad argued. I was only four but I'd never heard them arguing like that. I was scared. He wanted her to quit being a reporter. She didn't want to. She went to cover a story and was killed in a traffic accident." Scoop trailed off.

"My parents were both killed in a car accident." I wasn't trying to one up her but I wanted her to know I understood. There is enough guilt to go around. "I was in college. I never came home again. No reason to until yesterday."

"I wasn't that lucky. My dad never forgave her and absolutely refuses to discuss my going into journalism."

Scoop's intuitiveness would make her a hell of a reporter.

"He wants me to be a doctor." She made a face and I couldn't help laughing. "I don't like blood."

"Me neither." We laughed together and then it grew quiet.

"I'd better get going home before my dad sends out the police after me. He and Sam the Scam are buddies."

I wanted to ask about the moniker of the police chief but knowing her dad wouldn't be an ally was enough inside information for today.

I reached for the door handle.

Scoop looked around. "Where's your car?"

"Still at the Main Street Pub."

She looked puzzled. "I had a couple beers and walked home." That satisfied her and I didn't need others knowing about my midnight breakfast with the former homecoming queen although I wondered if that would be Monday's front-page headline.

Before I could push on the door to open it, the car revved into reverse backing out throwing me forward as it stopped. Then it took off throwing me against the back of the seat and I realized I still held the handle. Scoop drove toward Main Street.

"Hey, Dale Earnhardt. Could we slow to track speed, please?" I said it in a jest but her rapid driving made me a bit queasy.

"Oh, sorry." Scoop reddened as she slowed. She made a left then only a couple of blocks to the pub. She slowed as we neared the entrance. The basic-black rental sedan sported all four tires—the advantages of a small town.

She jerked the wheel back to the road as she turned in. She accelerated causing me to slam my head against the seat as she drove past the pub.

"What?" I voiced my annoyance at the crazy car antics of a teenager. "Dammit, this isn't the time for a childish show of temper."

She made no response as she executed a couple of quick turns. "Scoop, stop. Now!"

Before I could utter anything else, she almost made a U-turn, pulled into a garage and quickly shut the door.

As the last dregs of sunlight left the now dark garage, I found my voice. "If you wanted more of my reporting knowledge, you could have asked." I stumbled through the words hoping for lightness but I wondered if I'd been kidnapped.

My eyes tried to adjust to the dim interior and I heard Scoop's door open. The inside dome light helped illuminate a lawnmower, rakes and other equipment typically found in a suburban storage facility. I'd had enough. If this was one of Scoop's tricks to impress me, I wasn't buying it.

"What the hell is going on?" I climbed out of the car and faced her across the roof, her face in shadow.

"You hungry?"

Her questioned stopped my anger as I realized lunch had been forgotten in my attempt to get Scoop to spill, but the kidnapping still annoyed me.

I followed her into a large kitchen with yellow walls, oak cabinets and blue and yellow curtains lined the window over the sink.

She motioned for me to take a stool at counter that jutted into the room. I did. Scoop rummaged in the refrigerator and started setting out lunchmeat, condiments, lettuce, tomato and several ingredients I could only imagine. Next she added bread.

"Make yourself a sandwich? You like Faygo grape soda?"

I nodded and a two-liter joined the mix. An uneasy feeling hit my stomach. I was alone with a teenage girl and ripe for another scandal. I should get out of here and fast so I didn't waste any time making a Dagwood sandwich with the medley of ingredients. After the first bites I decided I could wait a few minutes to leave. I sipped the purple liquid. I ate a few more bites.

"Where's your dad?" I took another bite of my sandwich.

"Golfing at the Flatville Country Club. Every Saturday rain or shine."

Scoop put a small recorder on the counter. "Mr. Malone, I will be recording our interview."

I stared first at the recorder and then at Scoop.

"What interview? Why?" I realized Scoop hadn't made a sandwich.

"Mr. Malone, why are the police looking for you?" She sipped at her grape soda.

"The police aren't looking for me," I sputtered, then realized they may be.

"Don't lie to me. They were staking out your car at the bar." A smug look crossed her face.

"They were?" I thought back to the parking lot. I didn't see any police cars or anyone even sitting in a vehicle. The parking lot was empty except for my car.

"On the back side of the parking lot, across an alley is the usual spot for the cops to clock the Main Street traffic. Flatville's own speed trap. Except today the officers watched your car, their radar gun missing. Why?"

"I don't know. I'm not exactly a fan of the chief of police."

"Did you kill Trudy Harrison?" Her voice hard, challenging.

She would be good with a little training and that would start now.

"No and you should know that or you're one stupid girl. What would stop me from killing you to keep the information quiet? Did you ever think about that? A good reporter only confronts people in a public place where others can be witnesses if need be."

Red suffused Scoop's face.

"They want you for some reason. What is it?"

"Other than to make my life miserable, I don't know. This is off the record."

"No way. I want a big story. Show up those fools in the newsroom."

I wanted to walk out of the room and forget I had ever met Scoop. Getting kidnapped, questioned and then my own story stolen from me by a high school wannabe did not happen to Mitch Malone. I looked at Scoop, ready to jump down her throat and would have had we been in a real newsroom. The eyes stopped me. So earnest, excited but vulnerable too. I knew. I had lost my parents and buried myself in my work to forget the pain. I also endured grief from Biff and Bob. That pair would be vicious and unrelenting especially with someone without defenses.

I'd hate myself for this but saw no other way around it. "I promise we'll get this story together, share the credit." I stuck my hand out.

She cocked her head to one side thinking about any way I could get out of the deal.

"You'll keep your word?" She sounded skeptical. Couldn't say I blamed her with Biff and Bob as role models.

"What kind of reporter would I be if I broke my word? I would lose all my sources. A good source is worth his or her weight in gold. I won't back out."

She weighed my words and then came to a decision. She reached out and turned off the tape recorder. "What do the cops want with you?"

I decided to be honest with her. "They want to convict me of Trudy's murder." My voice caught on her name. I still couldn't believe she was dead.

"Why? If you didn't do it, wouldn't they want to catch who did?"

"In a perfect world, yes. But I grew up here and I never got along with the police chief. He may not believe I did it but arresting me gives him a certain satisfaction."

I saw her puzzled look.

"One of the first things you need to learn to be a good reporter is people don't always tell you the truth and they rarely do anything for the greater good. They always have ulterior motives."

Her eyes hardened. "That ain't honest."

I nodded my head. "That's the way it is." I also realized my handshake had put Scoop squarely in the face of danger. I had to think fast to figure out how to keep her safe.

I finished off my grape soda while she thought about what I said.

"So the big story here is whoever did kill her and why are the police covering it up."

I nodded again. "Scoop, we need to be careful. I don't want you caught up in their games. I need you to be my secret weapon. I don't want anyone to know we are working together."

I knew if she thought I was trying to protect her she would jump in and never look back. She was only a kid and I didn't need any more guilt if something happened to her. I knew Sam and Ram could be brutal, maybe even killers She didn't need to see the darker side of her father's friends.

"You can listen to what Biff and Bob have to say in the newsroom, maybe even eavesdrop on your father to find out what is going on. If anyone notices you, you pretend to be just curious. You can't tell anyone you and I are working on a story. A good reporter keeps all the facts to him or herself until they come out in print. That way they don't get scooped." I smiled. "Sorry about the pun."

"I've heard them all. I get it. You have to keep your cards close to your vest. I can do it."

"Ready for your first assignment?"

"Yes, sir." She saluted but had such a cocky smile I had to laugh.

"I need to call the Flatville Bed and Breakfast and see if the cops are staking out where I'm staying."

She pointed to the phone on the counter by the wall. She pulled a phone book out of the cupboard above the phone and looked up the number.

"Harold, Mitch here."

"Yes, Mary. What can I do for you?" Harold's voice replied.

"Are the police waiting for me?"

"Yes, we have your reservation all set. See you then." Harold hung up on me.

I stared at the phone.

"What's wrong?"

"The police are at the bed and breakfast." I searched my pockets and pulled out Clive's card.

I dialed and Clive answered on the first ring.

"I'm a wanted man," I said without preamble or identifying myself.

"Yes, I am aware of that. I was just going to call you. Turning yourself in is the best option. More controlled. Less of a chance you could get hurt."

"Okay. Can you meet me at the police station?"

"It would be better if I accompanied you. That way they can't stonewall me at the front desk."

I told him where I was.

"Scoop. I have to face the wolves and probably won't be able to connect with you until at least tomorrow." I pulled my new reporter's notebook from my back pocket and handed it to her. "Write down everything you hear that could possibly be related and make sure you note who said it.

"You want me to use your notebook? Thanks!"

"Remember we are partners, but you are the silent one. Don't get yourself into any trouble. Don't get caught eavesdropping. Safety is a reporter's number one concern. Theirs and others."

She nodded.

"Thanks for the lift today, partner." I held out my hand and we shook.

Chapter 11

SCOOP DROVE ME to Clive's office. I tried to shake the feeling that a target adorned my back as I turned up the walk of a small brick home that had been converted to office space. I felt sweat bead and run down my back. It could be from the hot sun or nerves. Glancing over my shoulder, I couldn't shake the feeling I'd be thrown to the ground and cuffed at any minute.

My concern mounted when I could see the courthouse and jail behind the office looming like a monolith. The courthouse oozed Southern charm with three-story, white pillars flanking the front entrance surrounded by lush green grass and flower beds comprising the city's center square. It was the community's figurehead, a beacon of welcome as espoused by the Chamber of Commerce, unusual for a small community so far north of the Mason-Dixon Line.

I opened the door and darted in following Clive's instructions. My breath whooshed out as the door clicked into place. I had made it. This paranoia ensured I would never follow a life of crime. The stress of being in the police crosshairs could make you crazy with the constant glancing around. I'd been chased by the feds and never felt this vulnerable, but these small town guys have itchy trigger fingers especially when stirred up by their chief. I couldn't help but wonder if there was more going on here than a simple murder. I tried to shake the feeling of impending doom that was exasperated by going from bright sunshine to a dimmer interior that had me momentarily blinded.

"Glad to see you," Clive greeted me heartily, holding out his hand which

I took. "Any problems?" He propelled me forward from the outer office into a room filled with afternoon sunshine.

"No." I wanted to add that I felt like everyone was watching me but resisted. I was Mitch Malone, Pulitzer-Prize-nominated reporter. I didn't get scared. Had returning to my hometown torn apart my psyche, my self confidence? I refused to regress to the bookish, shy boy I'd been. There would be no cowering to the police or to my cousin. I lifted my face to the warming sun from the window and rolled my shoulders letting the air-conditioned temperature cool my nerves. As I stretched, I felt some of the tightness release. I hadn't realized the baggage pull from this town made me hunch forward and vowed not to let it make me run or hide. This former shrimp of a kid refused to back down to the grade-school bully.

"This is how it is going to work," Clive motioned me to a brown leather chair in front of a dark wood desk that dominated the room. Forcing myself to return to my reporter instincts, I glanced around realizing we were in what would have been a dining room in an earlier lifetime. A large, multi-paned window was along one side with a view of a beautiful garden along the side of the home, err office. A chandelier above my head glinted in the sunlight banishing my insecurities and turning my resolve into a plan of action as I took the offered seat.

"I like to raise roses," he said noticing my attention on the flowers.

"Really?" An attorney that works in a rose garden? I wondered how good of an attorney he would be especially under the pressure of the police.

"I find it calms my mind, allows me to focus better on my work." He spoke slowly with rich tones that would make the Eureka County justice system take notice.

"Do you think I'm going to be arrested and charged with murder and have to sit in jail?" I jumped up and started toward the window then turned back to face Clive. I couldn't sit here and calmly talk about roses. I needed to know what was going to happen to me.

Clive stopped mid-sentenced and motioned to the chair. I sat.

"My apologies. This must be stressful on you." Again the soft, smoothing voice.

I couldn't sit still. My knees and legs were jerking like a two-year-old having to go to the bathroom.

"This case seems to have created quite a stir and has many paying close attention including some federal agencies though I'm not able to determine exactly what their interest is. I'm not sure if that is good or bad."

The Feds! I'd waltzed with them a time or two with both positive and negative results. I thought of Patrenka Peterson, who used her wiles to get the job done and then left town without a backward glance. Her partner, Sam. Were all bad cops named Sam? This one was on the take and nearly ended up getting me killed when I was on a hot story about terrorists.

I jumped up pacing back and forth struggling to get my scattered thoughts to focus. I forced myself to stop in front of the window attempting to calm my nerves. I felt like Alice who had dropped into Wonderland and found it anything but. Nothing seemed real or normal.

I watched the roses in full bloom swaying in the slight breeze. A bumble bee attempted to land on the petals buffeted by the current. I knew exactly how the bee felt. Success. The rotund insect that should never be able to fly had touched down. I moved from the window and returned to my chair. I had to keep focused like the bee or I would never find the honey or in this case, who had killed Trudy and why.

Clive watched me deal with my own demons.

Taking my seat again, I couldn't get sucked into the past. I needed a single-minded determination to solve the current problem. For the bee it had been landing on the flower petals. For me it was staying out of jail. My mind took off again. Could they lock me up? How could I do anything behind jail walls? I'd never truly faced the thought of being incarcerated. I worked with the police, not on the other side of the law. My agitation and panic was growing. I felt spurred into action. I leaned forward to rise.

"Mitch?" Clive's voice held concern as he grabbed my shoulder bringing me back from my dark thoughts and pushing me back into the chair. I hadn't realized he'd even risen or moved from behind his desk. So focused on my panicked thoughts.

"Yes?" I closed my eyes and shook my head to clear it out. "Sorry. I've never been behind bars unless it was for a short time for a story knowing I could call a guard at any time to get out."

"I understand. Let's look at the possibilities, shall we?" Clive's voice was like honey forcing my panic to recede.

I was Mitch Malone. I could go to jail if standing behind the First Amendment and the right of free speech. I needed to keep it in perspective. I was innocent. This was still America. I couldn't be held if I was innocent.

"When you go in for questioning, there is a chance they could arrest you on some charge from manslaughter to first degree murder. Even though it is a weekend, I imagine they will get a judge in to set bail."

Clive looked at me to see if what he was saying was sinking in. I nodded.

"With your connections they are going to make sure they are doing it by the book."

"What are the odds they have enough to charge me?"

"I'd say slim. They don't have a local lab for any tissue or fiber evidence. Everything would have to be sent out to the state police lab, but it is possible. We need to be prepared."

I nodded. I trusted Clive.

"Worst case is first degree murder. I doubt they could find a motive. You're here to teach seminars at the Flatville newspaper. Did you know Trudy was here?"

"I didn't know anyone was here. I haven't been back since college. It has been fifteen years. I didn't keep in touch with anyone. How could I possibly have a motive?"

"You didn't know it was your class reunion? You didn't get an invitation?" Clive pressed.

"I don't think so. I severed all ties when I left." I thought for a moment. "I didn't even want to come here for the seminars but I didn't have any choice."

"Did you ever date Trudy in high school?"

"No. She was Ram's girlfriend."

"Ram's your cousin?"

I nodded and Clive started scribbling on his legal pad. The scribbling fed my panic.

"What?" The word came out a little high pitched and I felt myself begin to stand. Hurdling across a table at the questioner was not going to score points in my judicial process.

"The oldest motive in the world: Love and jealousy."

"Jealous? Me? Of who?" This was so unfair. I grabbed the arms of the chair and started to push myself up. "I left this town and never had a reason to return. The first night I'm back someone gets killed and I'm to blame?" My voice cracked on the last word.

Clive raised his hand. "Mitch, you have to calm down. If they can get you to make an outburst, then they can show you have a propensity for violence." He used both his hands to demonstrate. "Take a deep breath." His hands came up from his waist along the side of his body to his chin. "Then let it out." His hands lowered. "You try."

I breathed in and out forcing myself to relax into the seat.

"You have to remain calm no matter what issues the prosecutor or the police raise. If he can show you have a temper, you could be held without bail."

I was a professional reporter. I could be calm. I needed to pretend I was covering a story and this wasn't about my life being spent behind bars.

"Let's talk bail. How much could you raise?"

I considered my finances. I could easily raise a couple of thousand but a murder charge would have a heftier bail. "What would they set bail at?"

"It varies depending on the judge and the risk of flight. You don't have any local connections?"

"No, not any more. I know a bail bondsman from Grand River who could help."

"That isn't going to work." Clive sighed and sat back in his seat.

"But I only live and work a couple hours away. I'm in the same state."

"It may work but you need someone with local connections and pull. It'll depend on the judge." Clive was deep in thought. "I don't see the bond going over half a million."

I gulped. "I couldn't come up with half a million."

"Could you raise $50,000? That would be ten percent."

I nodded, stunned. "I could take a loan against my retirement account but that would take a day or two to process and I couldn't even start until Monday.

"We will argue that you have no history of crime, the prosecutor's theory is half baked and you aren't a flight risk." Clive looked at me and the silence stretched.

I took one last deep breath and nodded.

"Any questions?"

I shook my head and couldn't help but have my chin sink into my chest.

I resigned myself to spending several nights in jail. Maybe I could do an exclusive about jail life. A first-person exclusive and I would win the bet. It was the only comfort I had.

Chapter 12

AS WE WALKED across the city square to the police station, I felt every eye looking at me but couldn't figure out from where. Even though my wrists hung at my side, not pulled behind with handcuffs, I felt the curiosity of those gazing at a condemned man. I'd done nothing wrong. My shoulders slid back, my head came up. Flatville would not defeat me. I would not run away.

Clive and I walked shoulder to shoulder as we took the five steps up and pulled on the door to city hall and police station. The police chief, another gentleman in a suit, and Sweeney in the same uniform he'd been in when he wanted to arrest me that morning, waited in the lobby.

The small lobby shrunk when we entered. Clive shook hands with each of the three but no one seemed interested in shaking my hand.

Clive made the introductions. I nodded at Sam and Sweeney.

"This here is Whitaker Evans, sheriff of Eureka County."

The sheriff held out his hand and I shook it, surprised by the firm shake and the calloused palm. "Pleasure to meet you, Mr. Malone."

I saw something in his eyes that set me at ease. Why did I feel this way? The blue eyes that sparkled like my friend, Dennis Flarity, on the Grand River Police Department or maybe the hands that said he wasn't afraid to work.

Sam scowled at the friendly greeting and that clinched the deal. The sheriff would see I got a fair hearing. Clive also seemed to relax.

"Gentlemen," Sam grounded out, "shall we move this way."

I thought we would be heading for an interrogation room but then realized that would be a tight fit with five people.

Instead we went down a hall to a conference room with an oval wood table big enough to seat twelve. Sam took the chair at one end and I took the other. Clive sat next to me and the officer next to Sam. The sheriff sat in the middle with the name-card "Mayor R. Malone" in front of him.

The sheriff tipped the sign toward him and read, then silently chuckled like it was the biggest joke. Glad to see someone not under the bully's thumb.

We all looked around at each other waiting for someone to make the first move. Sam moved his arm forward and the uniformed officer jumped up.

"We will be recording the conversation today." He pointed to a tape recorder on the table, leaned forward and started it. He withdrew a card from his pocket and read off my rights.

He also mentioned everyone in the room and Clive represented me. The formalities completed, the questioning began.

"Mr. Malone, could you tell us your whereabouts on Friday night?" The officer sat, his chair squeaking in protest.

I looked at Clive and he nodded.

"The Main Street Pub having a hamburger after completing my work at the newspaper." I glanced around and every eye except one centered on me. I squirmed, uneasy about being on the answering end of questions.

"About what time was that?"

"Five thirty, six o'clock."

"Did you have anything to drink?" The officer didn't look up from the yellow pad in front of him. Odd, he refused to make eye contact to gauge my reactions. So I watched him to determine if he didn't care, the questions weren't his or he hadn't rehearsed.

I looked at Clive. We'd discussed how much I'd imbibed. Clive said not to lie but not to say anything that implied I had been drunk or not in command of my faculties. He nodded.

"I had a beer with my burger." That statement was true but left out I'd had one before I'd eaten as well.

"What happened next?"

"I was joined by two colleagues from the newspaper and we chatted."

"Did you consume more alcohol?"

"I finished my beer with dinner." That wasn't a lie but I couldn't remember how many beers I'd had. I'd paid my tab with dinner and it only showed two beers. I'd paid for the rest in cash.

The questioning of my eating and drinking habits covered the next few hours including who I'd talked to and about what.

When I thought we were finishing, he would start from the top again but with a different angle. He attempted to make me contradict myself. I began to understand the concept of confessing to get it over with as he started from the top for the fourth time.

Sam enjoyed it even less. When he caught me looking in his direction, his teeth clenched. The endless questioning wore on his nerves. I felt good about that. If I had to endure this, then so did he.

Throughout the questioning, I'd glossed over my conversation with Scott. I didn't want to talk about Aaron or his death. The police couldn't be interested in an accidental death years ago.

The questions seemed to be nearing an end.

"What did you talk to Trudy about?" The officer's voice rasped, his throat dry.

"Nothing much. My work at the paper mostly." My tone a tad flippant, my brain ready to call it quits.

"Come now, Mitch," Sam's hard voice jolted me from my lackadaisical attitude. The bad cop routine began.

"You talked on and off for the evening with a beautiful woman and all you talked about was yourself? You didn't ask her any questions?" He leaned in closer, his eyes hardening.

"It was normal stuff you talk about with someone you haven't seen in years." The line of questioning baffled me. Why was Sam so interested when he had snoozed through the earlier answers like he hadn't listened?

"Trudy didn't invite you to the reunion so she could talk to you?" Sam pushed harder.

What would Trudy have wanted to talk to me about? I wasn't even in her crowd in high school. "No. I didn't even know it was the night of the reunion."

"Come on. Didn't you plan this little excuse of a seminar so you could come home on the newspaper's dime to meet Trudy, the girl you had a crush on during high school?"

How did Sam know I had a crush on Trudy? I hadn't told anyone that except for maybe Aaron and Scott years ago. Like I would still be interested years later. I had plenty of opportunities with women. Patrenka Peterson's image returned front and center. I needed to stop thinking about that hot FBI agent. I refused to talk about my love life or my lack of it to anyone. The absurdity made me want to laugh in a crazed humor.

I looked at Clive waiting for him to object to badgering his witness. He leaned back in his chair, relaxed, his fingers clasped together with the pointy fingers extended making the steeple of the church in the old nursery rhyme.

Silence followed and I realized the pregnant pause was waiting for my answer about Trudy.

"No." The answer came out louder than I liked and even Clive shifted in his seat. I knew this game. Emotional outbursts would start the nails closing the coffin of guilt and justify their single-minded focus.

"Come on, Mitch. Level with us." Sam's voice smooth, cajoling. "You arranged the seminars so that you could get another chance with Trudy. Admit it. Nothing wrong with that. Trudy was a beautiful girl. You tried to start something Friday night and she refused or worse. She laughed at you? All the years of frustration came bubbling out. It was an accident. Admit it, Mitch. We understand. It was an accident."

"What? No. You got it wrong. I wasn't interested in Trudy. I didn't want to even do the seminar. I didn't even want to come to Flatville. I never wanted to return to Flatville." My voice rose in anger, then I felt Clive's hand squeeze my wrist.

I leaned back in my chair. I hadn't realized I had moved to within a foot of Sam over the table with the vehemence of my statement.

"How…" Sam started.

"Gentlemen, how much longer do you intend on questioning my client?"

Clive's interruption of Sam's next question allowed me time to regroup. I forced myself to sit back and appear relaxed.

Sam tensed at the interruption, shooting imaginary bullets at Clive's head. The bad cop tasted the blood of a confession with only a few more stabbing questions to my manhood. Somehow Sam realized his murderous aggression and exerted his control by backing from my face.

I looked around the table and discovered the sheriff, a blank poker face covered his features. I tried to school my features in the same unemotional façade. I wondered if he played hold'em at the Moose.

"When did you leave the bar?" Sam demanded.

"Around eleven, I believe." I hadn't remembered looking at my watch.

"Did you drive back to where you were staying?"

Round five of questioning but not from a disinterested voice but one who hated me and the feeling was mutual.

"No." I decided on short answers. I didn't want to give Sam too much information and make him think he broke me during questioning. Clive had suggested such a strategy. Never lie but only give them as much as they ask for. He advised I disclose I took Trudy to breakfast. They were bound to find a witness somewhere to come forward. A big news event like murder drew all the crazies out to be a witness. Sam wouldn't worry about anything like the truth for a conviction.

"What did you do when you left the bar?"

"I intended to drive myself to the bed and breakfast where I was staying." I glanced around the other faces to see if they thought this a waste of time like I did. The sheriff had his hands behind his head leaning back in the chair like he enjoyed the show and knew he had the winning hand.

"And?" Sam pushed on the table, rising out of his seat leaning over to get closer to me. His breath spewed the aftermath of the onions from his lunch.

"I heard something by the dumpster and went to investigate." I was flippant. A good reporter always checked out oddities, but I volunteered too much information, ground not covered by the good cop. I refused to disclose Trudy cowered behind the garbage container.

Sam pressed sensing weakness. "What was it?"

"Trudy was crying."

"What did she say?" His question in rapid-fire mode.

"Nothing much."

Clive leaned in ready to stop me. We finally saw what the sheriff wanted.

"Really? You find a beautiful woman you want to get in the sack broken and vulnerable and she doesn't say much?"

He paused for a minute shaking his head. He jabbed at my manliness to get a rise out of me but Trudy's memory meant more than Sam's opinion of my sexual prowess.

"Come off it, Mitch. Quit lying. What did she say? Woman can't wait to tell a willing ear what is bothering them. We all know that." Sam glanced around at the others in the room as if to get their agreement. Satisfied he turned back to me. "What was she upset about?"

I agreed with him. Women always poured out their problems. I used that effectively as a reporter.

"I don't know." Trudy's sobs weren't intelligible. After she'd calmed down, I understood the words, but the meaning didn't make any sense.

"Come on, Mitch. You claim to be a prize-winning journalist and you couldn't get why a damsel was in distress? That doesn't say much for your skills." Again that attack on my manhood expanding to my professionalism. Sam may be good at breaking criminals but not me.

"Sorry, no." I clasped my hands together on the table, my tone polite. I smiled at Sam to let him know his technique failed. I mastered the game.

Sam reddened and I hoped his blood pressure climbed. Maybe I could break him. Instead he sat back in his seat and nodded to his officer.

I felt sorry for the officer who cleared his throat and looked frantically through his notes trying to figure out what to ask next. He'd been caught up in the cliffhanger for an old Western movie drama.

"You couldn't make out what Ms. Harrison was saying?" Sam's second stuttered out.

"Correct. She seemed inebriated."

The officer shuffled through his papers again, clearly at a loss of where to take this. "What did you do then?"

Nice basic question when you don't know what to ask. I'd used this ploy as a cub reporter but it never worked well. I figured I'd give the officer a little more to work with.

"I couldn't leave her there as upset as she was. I was afraid she would hurt herself. It had already looked like she had fallen." I thought back to that night and how Trudy looked. How could anyone be so cold as to leave her when she was so upset? Then I thought of the killer and knew someone could.

"So you took her to the woods to calm her down?" The officer broke into my thoughts.

"What? No." I'd been distracted, tired from matching wits with Sam. I wanted this over. "She was trying to get in her car and in no shape to drive. She couldn't get her keys in the lock. I drove her to breakfast to sober her up."

"Where?"

"McDonalds in Bellville by the highway."

"What did she talk about?" Sam broke into the questioning.

I thought for a minute. What had she talked about?

"Don't tell me she didn't say anything you could understand while you were waiting for your food? What did she talk about?" Sam's blood pressure was on the rise. I could hear him start to lose control. I looked at Clive.

"Gentleman, how much more questioning do you have? My client has been more than cooperative but I sense we are going in a different direction now," Clive's mahogany voice attempted to sooth the savage beast raging in police chief's eyes.

Sam pounded on the table. "We were getting to the heart of it."

Clive started to rise. "This is no longer sounding like a civilized matter."

Clive faced down the police chief, glad he was my attorney. Clive didn't fear the men in blue.

The sheriff leaned forward and spoke for the first time. "Gentlemen, please. Only a couple more questions. I see some hostility here between two people who may hold old grudges. How about I finish the questioning and we can all get on home. Shall we?" The unexpected Southern drawl broke the stalemate with neither side losing face.

I liked the sound of being able to get this over with and not be incarcerated. Maybe the sheriff could be an ally or better yet could feed me some information on the investigation.

Everyone nodded. The sheriff pulled his right leg up onto his lap and looked like he was talking with an old friend. His gesture made my reporter instincts go into hyper drive. The sheriff may seem like a good ole boy from the South but I sensed a tiger lurked underneath the relaxed exterior that would tear me limb from limb if given the slightest provocation. Sam may be mean but not the smartest fish in the pond. The sheriff glided like a shark and I'd best not swim without goggles to see my way or I would be lost in a murky jail cell.

"Mr. Malone, where were you between three and five this morning?"

I looked at Clive. He shrugged his shoulders.

"I was at the Flatville Bed and Breakfast. Sleeping." I was measuring each of my words making sure I didn't open myself up for any discrepancies.

"Can anyone confirm that?"

I thought for a minute wondering if Harold heard me return. Before I could formulate an answer, Sam stood and walked over to me.

The good cop's voice came at me from across the table. "Mitch Malone, you are under arrest for the murder of Trudy Harrison." I focused on the words under arrest when Sam's hands pulled me out of my chair. He forced my arms up and patted me down making the process as demeaning as possible. The police chief pushed me forward so from the waist up I blended into the table. The cold steel surrounded my wrists.

Sam bent low and whispered: "See if you can get an award for this from a jail cell."

I wanted to be indignant and proclaim my innocence but speech failed me.

The key actor in a B-rated movie had to play out the miscarriage of justice in order for the true criminal to be unmasked.

I submitted to the rough hands yanking me back to vertical. A strange calm settled over and I was an observer, not a participant although I did feel the pinch of the too-tight cuffs.

Clive patted my shoulder and I nodded in his direction to convey my control at being locked away. Maybe jail would give me a new perspective on what made Flatville tick or at least these civil servants. I couldn't think about how long I would be behind bars but told myself it wouldn't be long especially with Clive at my back. The story would be worth it.

My arm jerked as another officer pulled me toward the door. I walked out, head held high. No emotion. Sam pulled on my other arm from behind forcing me to stop. I looked over my shoulder and I saw hate in Sam's face. Why would he hate me? I hadn't been around for years. Steel-toed boots connected with my calf. I wanted to scream with the pain but again calm settled over my body. I glanced around the lobby area to see if anyone had seen the abuse I had taken.

I spotted Biff on the other side of the information counter. He held a small camera out from his chest and a blinding flash made everyone pause. We continued on. Mitch Malone's arrest would be the feature of Monday's newspaper and would be the occasion for a rare color photo on the front page.

Chapter 13

THE INJUSTICE OF it all. Would I be condemned without a trial? Sam pulled my arm offsetting my balance. I stumbled as another kick hit my shin strategically toed to be invisible and the police were helping me by not letting me fall. The oldest trick in the book. I wondered if I would survive the incarceration.

We left the small police station by a side door and walked across the village square. I could see Biff running to get in front of us. The camera clicked and another photo taken of the award-winning journalist who found himself in the middle of murder.

Would my friends believe it? I thought of Dennis Flarity, my friend at the Grand River Police Department. Would he think twice? A smile broke unconsciously from my lips as I thought about Elsie Dobson. She would believe in my innocence and would be kicking Sam in the shin if she thought it would get me out of jail and then for good measure would hit him over the head with her purse. Maybe I would get a batch of cookies with a file inside of them delivered to the jail.

Thinking of cookies made my stomach rumble and the sun dipped behind a cloud casting a grayness to the area. I glanced around again and saw Biff queuing up for another photo as Sam tightened his grip. Maybe we could get a police brutality shot. Sam's leg came back and I did a stutter step as if I had already stumbled moving my right leg out of the boot's trajectory. Sam pitched forward as the flash blinded everyone again.

"Remove that camera," Sam growled to another officer who headed in Biff's direction. So much for my evidence if Sam seizes the camera. Before the officer was halfway to Biff, he must have sensed his intentions and turned and speed-walked across the green in the direction of the newspaper. Maybe Biff did have some instinct for a story or maybe it was the will to survive. Either worked for me, if the photo showed Sam winding up for a kick.

As we entered the Sheriff's department, my eyes were momentarily blinded with the dim interior before we entered the booking area with two rows of fluorescent lights in the ceiling that seemed like thousands of watts compared to the low-lighted entry.

The brown uniformed deputy behind the desk stood as I approached along with my entourage. The sheriff turned to Sam. "We can handle it from here."

Sam started to snarl but then closed his mouth. "Notify me of the arraignment."

The sheriff nodded and watched as the boys in blue disappeared out the door we had entered.

"You aren't going to give us any trouble are you, Mr. Malone?"

I shook my head.

"Good. Buzz, remove these cuffs."

I rubbed my wrists as the blood started flowing back into my hands. I was searched again and fingerprinted. My belt, shoes, wallet, watch, camera, phone, notebook, pen, and spare change disappeared into a large yellow envelope.

"So tell me, Mitch, I can call you Mitch?" The sheriff leaned on the booking counter. "What have you done that has put a burr into our dear police chief's butt?"

By the way he said "butt," I knew there was no love lost between the two local law enforcement agencies. He invited confidences. I hesitated wondering if this was a variation on the good-cop, bad-cop routine. Or if the sheriff wanted to put it to the police chief. I decided it didn't matter. I could repay the bruises on my shins.

"I've been on Sam's list since high school. Never expected it to escalate to hand cuffs." I rubbed my wrists again. "So tell me what my prospects are?" If he could pump me for info, I could do the same. The sheriff motioned me to stand in front of a screen with lines across it. Another flash completed my mug shot.

"We're looking for a judge now to get you arraigned, hopefully by tomorrow morning so bail can be set and you can get out."

"You think they will set bail?" I leaned on the counter and looked him in the eye.

"You never know. Depends on the judge." The sheriff looked off my left shoulder.

"Any chance I can get my notebook so I can keep myself occupied?"

"We'll see."

The deputy that took my prints joined us and the moment of friendship was gone. I was led away to a cell near the booking desk.

I couldn't help shivering when the cell door slammed shut. I checked my accommodations. Silver toilet in the corner, two bunks along one wall and not much room to turn around. I thanked my stars it looked recently disinfected. I sat awkwardly on the bottom bunk with my head nearly touching the top, nearly forcing me to lean forward.

I sat and waited for a few minutes but realized it wasn't my style.

I walked to the door and looked out. I could see six cells and I assumed a second cell was beside me. I mentally noted each detail for a future story.

"Hey, buddy, got a smoke?" The voice was raspy and came from my left.

"Sorry no." I heard feet shuffling and figured that would be the extent of the conversation. I was wrong.

"What're you in for?"

I heard paper ripping. I didn't know what to answer. Was this a jailhouse plant looking for a lighter sentence in exchange for testimony on what I said?

"A trumped up charge."

I heard a cough deep in the throat and saw what looked like a spittle ball fly out into the center hallway area.

"Me too."

How convenient. I was tired of everyone wanting a piece of me.

"Don't go." His voice dropped even deeper and I could barely hear him.

"I heard you were a reporter for a big city paper. You've got to help me. I've been sitting here for two days. I ain't even gotten my phone call."

I heard the clang of the door and I thought I heard "later" from the neighboring cell. The same booking officer entered the hall. He had my notebook with him and tossed it through the bars.

He left and I heard the voice again. "Are you going to help me?"

I was a reporter confined to a jail cell. That didn't mean I couldn't work on another story. "Sure. Let's start with your name."

"Vince Carter."

"Tell me how you got to be here."

"I wasn't doing anything. I'm down on my luck and got a part-time job at the Flatville Country Club weeding the flower beds, making sure they look nice. I'm supposed to do my work at night so no one can see me. That works for me because it is so hot during the day, I couldn't take that." He paused for a breath and then let out a cough that seemed to rattle around inside before it finished.

"Go on."

"Two nights ago I worked on a bed out by the fifth fairway. It's the one where they have those condos surrounding the green. The flowers separate the course from the condo property. I'm lying there pulling weeds on account of my back not being in too good a shape."

I wondered if that was the whole truth. Was he looking in windows? Casing the places to see which were not occupied so he could relieve them of some belongings?

As if he sensed my thoughts. "Honest. I was just there pulling weeds and pulling off the bloomed flowers so they will continue to blossom." His voice changed to a more confident tone without boasting. "I know how to take care of flowers. They bloom under my touch. My Maw had a greenhouse until the bank took it."

"I believe you." I didn't but wanted to get the story out. At this rate I could be here for five years and not hear the whole thing.

"I may have dozed off or just been intent on my work, but I suddenly heard voices. I didn't pay them no mind at least not at first. Their heads were pushed close together like lovers, then I realized it was two men. They talked about some woman or something causing problems. Said something like 'Trudy doesn't want to keep our secret anymore. She refused to go to the reunion with me.'"

That perked up my ears. They had to be talking about Trudy Harrison.

There couldn't be two Trudy's in Flatville. I didn't want my source to sense my enthusiasm so I tried to keep my voice neutral and bored. "Did you happen to see who was talking? Did you know them?"

"One was a big guy but I couldn't see much on account it was dark. I tried to get a look at them."

That comment sounded fishy. Why? Was this guy just trying to make up a story to get a deal and get out of jail?

"The other guy was the same guy who brought you in."

"Which one?" I said the words too quickly, a rookie mistake. Vince started with his demands.

"Can you get me out? I wasn't even arrested properly."

"Tell me who you saw or it doesn't mean anything." I wondered if he was making this up. It could be easy to do. The whole town knew of Trudy's murder. A little guessing, a little supposition and Vince angling for a get-out-of jail-free card.

"The wiry guy with dark hair. Isn't he the police chief? What would he be doing talking about the dead girl before she was dead? That's why I'm here. You have to get me out before I disappear." His voice sounded younger now. I wish I could see him, look at his eyes, his posture. He knew something that scared him but was it about Trudy?

"Buddy, I'm in jail just like you. I'm not sure I can do anything. If I get out, I'll look into it."

"Is that all you can do?"

"Afraid so." I closed my notebook and went back to my bunk, laying on it. I was in a mine field and didn't know where to turn or who to trust. Worst yet I began to question my instincts as a reporter. My eyes dropped as exhaustion took over with too little sleep and too much stress.

Chapter 14

"ALL RISE." THE bailiff said the words with listlessness. For me they were dreaded. This hearing should be the beginning of the quest for guilt or innocence but for me it would be the end, marked guilty. No trial. No defense. Gone.

For some reason that made me think of Aaron. Aaron had been in my life one day and gone the next. Would Mitch Malone be gone by the end of the day? I hoped Aaron had gone to a better place. Me, I wasn't going to be so lucky. Thrown in a cell and the key would disappear. Sam and Ram would make sure of it.

Sure the law said everyone had a right to a fair trial but in Flatville, a fair trial was only if you knew someone and I didn't know anyone. I thought of Vince, still in his cell. No one cared or knew where he'd gone. I glanced at Clive and he was looking ahead. I couldn't read his emotions. I glanced around surprised to see a packed courtroom. It only held about fifty people but every seat looked taken.

It was Sunday morning, a special session of court. I'd spent the night in jail. I'd slept for about five hours but woke around three only to doze off and on listening to Vince's coughing and snoring cycle for the rest of the morning until I was given some breakfast and told to get ready for court.

The judge entered from the left, a door near the raised oak dais that commanded all attention at the front of the room. A woman sat in a small wooded cubicle in front of the judge and would be in charge of recording every word said.

"Be seated." The voice was stern and oddly familiar. I wondered if every judge was given voice lessons to sound the same. I wanted to chuckle at my bizarre musings. I'll get Biff and Bob right on that exposé.

I needed to get myself under control. I'd never responded to stress before with silly humor. I tried to make myself appear serious as I took my seat. I connected with the stern eyes of the judge, crystal clear blue eyes and felt a jolt to my toes.

I knew those eyes. It was the president of Faber College at least he held the position when my parents taught there. What was his name? I looked at the nameplate. The honorable Judge Thomas H. Roosevelt, a descendent of President Theodore Roosevelt but he never claimed any blood with Franklin. I never knew why. I never cared. His name graced every one of the guest lists for my parent's social functions, dry affairs where I dressed in a miniature suit and a bow tie when bow ties were far from style. I'd bow and shake hands if the adult initiated it. Mr. Roosevelt always insisted on shaking my hand with such a firm grip I always saved him for last because my hand hurt afterwards.

All this sped through while the eyes continued to lock on mine. My chair creaked as I pushed back.

Clive's whisper penetrated the terror. "What's wrong?"

"The judge was a friend of my parents."

"That could help." His voice soothing.

"I don't think so."

The judge nodded to the prosecution's table. A man I thankfully didn't recognize stood up and addressed the judge. "In the case of Green County versus Mitchell A. Malone. Mr. Malone is charged with first degree murder in the death of Trudy Harrison."

"How does the defendant plead?" The voice boomed as if on stage and even the cheap seats deserved to hear every word.

"Not guilty, your honor." Clive's voice was strong. He'd warned me earlier not to say a word. He would handle all the talking.

"Noted." The judge said curtly. "Bail?"

"The county requests the defendant be held without bail your honor." The tone of the prosecutor lackluster, just another case. I was offended.

"The defendant hadn't seen the victim in twenty years. He is well known and has been employed for several years. To incarcerate him until we come to trial would be an expense that is a waste of taxpayers' money. He is in town for work and is a face that is recognized across the state. He will not run. I request that he be released on his own personal recognizance."

"Your honor, the defendant was only in town less than twelve hours when he committed a heinous murder and then callously dumped the body. We cannot chance another horrendous crime." The prosecutor warmed to his subject but the judge silenced him with a look over his half-moon, reading glasses.

"Mr. Malone." The judge commanded and I looked up. "Do you have anything to say on your own behalf?"

Clive shrugged his shoulders.

"I didn't do this, your honor. I'm not going anywhere until my name is cleared. I believe in the criminal justice system. I will be found not guilty." The words tumbled out in one breath.

The judge nodded. "Bail is set at one million dollars. Court's adjourned." The gavel banged. The judge was out the door and into his office before the bailiff could say "all rise."

Clive turned to the prosecutor who was gathering up his papers. They shook hands. A deputy approached me. "Mr. Malone, I need to put you back in cuffs to return to the jail until bail can be arranged." He seemed to apologize. Was he a fan of my byline or another attempt by the sheriff to get me to confess.

I turned to Clive. "I don't have a million dollars."

"Don't need it. You will only need ten percent. The bondsman will front the rest."

While I covered hundreds of arraignments, I had never been on the other end to know how the bail arrangements were made. That might make an interesting story when I got back to Grand River, if I got back to Grand River.

"Where am I going to get a hundred-thousand dollars, especially on a weekend?"

"Do you own any property?"

"My condo but I still have a mortgage. I have a 401K but not sure bail is one of the approved uses for an early withdrawal." I'd tried to laugh but it came out hollow and scratchy.

"I'd be happy to provide the surety needed for Mitch's bail."

Richard A Malone, Sr., Ram's father, shook Clive's hand. "A Malone has never spent more than a night in jail and Mitch here isn't going to break that streak."

"Thanks." I didn't know what to say. It was a generous gift but an insult in the giving. But that is how I remembered Ram's family. Help you up with one hand and slap you with the other. Nothing had changed there either.

The deputy cleared his throat. I turned and held my hands out for the cuffs. It didn't bother me to put them on now, knowing I wasn't staying. I'd be released. I wanted to skip and do a high-five. Then I would be under arrest for attempted escape. I tried to keep my happy feelings from getting out of jail under control.

"Son, I know you didn't do this." My uncle squeezed my shoulder like a vise. "Ram and I will do all we can to see you are cleared."

"Thank you, sir." The deputy escorted me from the courtroom.

How much would he help if he knew I considered Ram the prime suspect?

Chapter 15

"MALONE, ARE YOU in?" Harold asked to get my attention.

I was in all right. In over my head. Why had I let Harold talk me into the Sunday night poker tournament at the Moose Lodge? He said something about collecting the local scuttlebutt. All I was collecting was debt. My chips were disappearing at an alarming rate.

What I thought would be a chatty night of locals talking about who killed Trudy had turned into a lot of talk about last fall's dismal football season, both the Detroit Lions and the Flatville Cougars. Players and positions were discussed in great detail leading to optimism this would be a good season for both teams.

What I didn't know was how they could be discussing football when the community had its first murder in twenty years. I'd left this town years ago but thought murder ought to rate at least a couple of snippets.

I threw a chip into the middle of the table. I heard a cough. It was Harold who gave me a nod of the head. I threw another chip into the middle. He nodded.

The dealer tossed two cards to everyone and I lifted a corner. Two aces.

I was sitting at an oval table with nine other guys. I was bluffing that I knew how to play. I would only be out the thirty dollar entrance fee if I lost within the first thirty minutes. If I found out anything, it would be money well spent. If not, it would be relaxing, at least according to Harold who sat on my left. There were five tables filled mainly with men playing Texas hold 'em poker. A baseball cap pulled low over my eyes disguised my features.

If I was taking a survey, poker participants would be a good cross section of the Flatville population sitting at what could have passed for pool tables except they were oval and had no pockets for the eight-ball to be sunk. Young and old, rich and poor. Only four women sat at the tables including one on my right. She'd won the last pot.

The bet was back to me and I had to make a decision. I tossed in six chips and suddenly I had all eyes on the table. Three cards were turned up on the table — A two, three and king were the flop. Guys on each end of the table groaned. I still had a pair of aces. The bet came around again and I was pleased to see the pile in the center grow. A couple folded but the woman was in as were the guys on each side of the dealer.

The next card turned was a nine. I saw a subtle nod from the dealer's left as he lifted his two cards and released them. The guy on the other side of the dealer clenched his teeth then released them. Another round of betting had me trying to figure if the first guy was holding more than a pair of nines or threes. I tossed in another stack of chips.

"That murder sure is something, ain't it?"

I looked over my shoulder at the table behind me from where the voice had come. I received another elbow in my side and turned back. The dealer had turned an ace giving me three. I threw another stack of chips into the pot leaving me with a single stack left.

"What a shame. Trudy was a real looker."

Again my attention bounced to the other table. I wanted to listen but knew I would be caught if I didn't pay attention to my hand.

"Classy too," drifted to my ears.

Another round of betting and two of the players on each side of the dealer went all in. I looked at my cards.

"Was hoping to ask her out." Another added then someone whistled.

I pushed all my chips in. Either I would win big or I would be out and free to listen to the conversation. A winning hand any way you looked at it.

"Nice too, but you never saw her out anywhere."

The guy who grimaced had a pair of twos and a pair of nines. The woman beside me had three threes. I flipped my aces. The smiley guy by the dealer tossed his cards on the table. They flipped over showing a pair of kings but three kings wouldn't beat my aces.

Suddenly hands slapped me on the back and chairs scraped. Break time and two of the players were out. I moved on to the next stage of the tournament and wanted to be at the table talking about the murder.

Everyone stood up and several from the table behind me were putting on their jackets. Were they leaving?

"Smoking," Harold whispered in my ear.

I wasn't a smoker but I wanted to hear the conversation and hoped Trudy stayed the subject.

I followed the group out the back door. A picnic table littered with burn marks had a large cigarette disposal at the end. The boys gathered around and the only sound was the rattle of the lighters before bursting into flame. Breaths inhaled and then out.

"Tough night," a voice said.

"Yup. How about them Tigers?" another added.

I felt a nudge on my arm and I looked to a guy beside me with close-cropped blond hair and striking blue eyes that I bet had broken hearts. He held out a pack of cigarettes.

I took one. I didn't smoke but I could look like it when I needed to blend in or show I had a bad streak when talking to hookers or drug dealers. I tapped the filter end a couple of times.

He fired his own lighter and held it out. I put the cigarette in my mouth and inhaled to get it lit. Voices murmured but I couldn't catch the conversation.

"Wayne, what's up with that girl they found?"

I inhaled at the question and then had a fit of coughing.

Now this was more like it. I looked at my feet trying not to appear interested and catch my breath.

"Think we have a guy. He's from out of town." The voice was the blond who offered me a cigarette. Did he know I was that guy? I adjusted my cap lower over my face.

"Did he do it?"

A burst of chuckles rumbled.

"We wouldn't have arrested him, would we?" Sarcasm dripped from his lips with the inane question. He took another long drag from his cigarette.

"Was it true that she was beaten and tossed in the river?" This from a young kid who was barely old enough to get in the adult game.

I naturally looked at my hands. No bruised knuckles. A point in my favor.

"Don't believe everything you hear." Wayne's voice was cajoling like he was talking to a two-year-old.

"How was she killed?" Excitement tinged the voice.

Wayne exhaled slowly through his teeth. Patience wasn't his strong suit, similar to Sam in that regard. "Autopsy isn't back yet." The way he said it made me think he was picturing the broken lifeless body.

I'd not seen Trudy but had viewed other bodies and it was a picture that hung with you.

"This guy should be hanged if he comes to town to kill the prettiest homecoming queen ever." This from a guy who looked familiar. I wondered if he was in my high school class.

I inhaled quickly and then blew the smoke straight out to hide my face in the cloudy air.

Murmurs all around sounded in agreement. Great, if they found out I was the suspect, I would be hung on the nearest tree.

I started to turn back inside where Harold could protect me.

"I can't understand why they chucked her body in the river. It's been so dry, the current is almost nonexistent. Lots of other places they could have hidden the body or better yet buried it. Why leave it where it would be discovered?" This from a gray-haired guy down from me in the semi-circle around the table.

Was Trudy's body found in the river? No one had said anything about that. All I could picture was Aaron's body in the eddy. Was that why there wasn't any evidence at the bluff for Scoop and me to find?

"Maybe he wasn't familiar with Flatville and didn't think anyone would be out in the woods." Wayne warmed to his role as the source of murder information.

"It's June. Everyone goes to the park. Killer would have to be daft not to realize that." Again the older guy.

"Killers aren't the smartest people. Otherwise they wouldn't be caught. I'm sure our ten minutes are up." Wayne turned and headed in.

"Murder doesn't make any sense," the gray-haired guy took a last drag of his cigarette and put it into the small hole at the top of the cigarette disposal.

I couldn't agree more but didn't voice my thought. I still could get valuable information tonight if the murder continued as the prime conversation topic.

Others followed suit and headed in. I followed last, deep in thought nearly forgetting to dispose of my cigarette. So the murderer wasn't bright. It couldn't be me. I smiled to myself knowing that logic wouldn't get far in court.

As I looked over the tables, the players had all been shuffled and one table stood empty. I searched the tables but the only thing that told the tale was the pile of chips and I wasn't given the treasure map to find my seat. I wondered if they found out I was the suspect and booted me from the game. I glanced around looking for escape routes and saw none except the way I had come. A half-dozen guys stood talking near the entry. I readjusted my cap a bit higher to see more of the room.

Harold waved from the far side of the room. He nodded at the chair in front of him and a large pile of chips. I headed in that direction.

Wayne, the cop, was at the end of the table with his back to the door. The older guy to my left was now next to the dealer. No one else looked familiar. The chips started flying to the center. The stakes were higher but I was anxious to get out. I didn't think it would be healthy for me to stay if they found out I was the suspect.

Winning the last hand before was beginner's luck. I could lose a bunch of chips in a hurry and be done. Harold was already out. He should know better. He doesn't have a poker face.

He left my side after we started and wandered to the other two tables and chatted with people seemingly at home.

The deal came around and I kept betting and barely looking at my cards. For the next hands, I won. I wanted to lose and be gone. The table was smaller as three people had gone all in and lost to my hands.

It was me, the cop, the old guy and a young kid at the opposite end of the table from Wayne. Talking had been kept to a minimum and mostly about chips and angst at losing hands. I'd kept my mouth shut and my head down.

I glanced around at the three other tables in the tournament. They had three or four at them as well. A couple other tables had started with people who were out of the tournament paying for chips in cash.

Had I been in a different town, different circumstances, this might have made a great story. A portion of the proceeds went to various charities each week that provided the volunteers who sold the chips and collected the entrance fees. Today I was looking for information to save my own neck.

My stomach sank. My old buddy Sam walked in. I would be flogged from this group. I sunk lower in my seat hoping to remain hidden. I returned the baseball cap to block my profile.

Harold had seen him too. He walked nonchalantly over to my side to block Sam's view. Sam started over and bent down to catch the ear of the officer who had been so vocal about the murder. I watched as anger entered his eyes but he kept them lowered to avoid detection by his superior officer.

Wayne started to argue but Sam cut him off with a curt word whispered in his ear. The underling shoved all his chips into the middle causing the ordered piles to cascade like dominoes across the green surface.

He waited for the last card to be turned. He threw his cards down on the table, pushed back and walked out the door.

I wanted to know what happened.

The old guy racked in the pot with two pair. "His loss is my gain," he cackled.

"Why'd he leave?" The words slipped out bringing all eyes to mine at the table.

"You ain't from around here, are you?" The old guy gave me the once over.

I shook my head. "Here for work for the next week."

"That there was the police chief forcing one of his officers to do some lame errand or such."

"Can he do that?" I knew Sam but didn't think he could stay in his job with the city based on the behavior I'd seen.

"Yes. When you have the city council in your back pocket, you can run the town." The old guy didn't sound like he was joking.

We returned to silence as the cards were dealt and the ante was in.

Chapter 16

AN HOUR LATER I was still in the tournament. The stakes were high with only four of us left at a single table. Two other tables were playing for cash. Harold played for a few hands and then watched me. It was way past his bedtime. I was exhausted and knew I was in this tournament through no skill on my part but the luck of some good cards. I'd gone all in on a couple of hands and the river card, the last card turned, played right into my hand. Some days you couldn't lose or was it skill?

The off-duty officer hadn't returned and conversation turned to rainfall amounts and the county fair in a couple of weeks. I planned to go all in on the next hand regardless of my cards. Time for this day to be over before it was the next day.

"Harold, has that developer submitted any plans for all that land?" Harold was back standing behind me and this from a guy who was wandering around having left the game at another table.

"Not yet. We figure he has purchased about thirty acres adjacent to the river. No one has heard a thing and the township hasn't seen a plan either." Harold's voice was interested but fatigued.

I had to get out of this game. I moved my chips into the center ring. I hadn't even looked at my hand. I was hoping for a little bad luck.

"I heard it was some big-city developer wanting to put a resort on the river and cater to the fishing crowd." The guy was now on the opposite side of the table.

"Don't believe everything you hear, Burt." Harold chuckled.

"Sam said someone submitted the paperwork for a liquor license and he was doing a background check."

"That may be but until they submit the plans to the city for approval by the planning commission, I won't have any information." Harold's voice lost its humor, exhaustion making him snapish.

Another card was flipped and I watched the other three. One guy folded and the other two increased the stakes.

"We sure could use some tourist business. Some restaurants and bars are barely keeping the doors open."

This guy wouldn't let it drop. Harold didn't want to discuss it. "Saw the hardware store was putting in a line of fishing equipment."

The bidding was around again and finally the river card of what I hoped was my last hand. The guy on my right had put all his chips in as well.

I picked up my cards and I had a two and a jack. I looked at the flipped cards relieved to see that nothing matched. Nodding to the other players I rose from the table intent on leaving.

"Sir." I didn't pay any attention but Harold grabbed my arm.

"Sir, you tied for third. Take this to the cashier and collect your winnings." The dealer handed a similar tag to the guy on my left then returned to shuffle the cards.

I looked at the red laminate tag in my hand. Tied for third place. Not bad for not even trying. I headed to the cashier.

The guy on my left arrived at the same time. While the cashier counted out forty bucks for each of us, the man in a green t-shirt held out his hand.

"Jeff Smith. Good to meet you."

"Mitch. Good game." I didn't want to give out my last name. I was almost out of there until this hometown boy wanted to know who had tied with him.

Harold was at my side and we beat a hasty retreat to his car. The good thing about Flatville was you're always home within minutes. He barely said goodnight before ambling to his rooms somewhere on the ground floor.

Chapter 17

I ADDED A tie to my normal line up of button down shirt and jeans and changed my leather bomber jacket for a navy blazer. I wasn't sure why I needed more formal wear except that I figured it would lend credibility to what I said. The first day of my four-hour sessions began today and would fill the afternoon. Why had I agreed to return to Flatville? I knew. It was ego.

I could see the clock tower on top of the courthouse over a block away as it chimed nine o'clock. I wanted to see how the newsroom functioned to get a better idea of how to focus my points. I came in the front door and went to my left into the newsroom. The reporters were on deadline. They wouldn't thank me for any interference. In an hour, maybe longer, their stories completed and moods would relax. Now I could observe them without them realizing it as they single-mindedly finished off their stories.

Bob was hunched over his keyboard typing furiously. Biff's desk was empty. If he covered the police beat he was out getting the weekend news. I looked through the glass window on the door to the news editor who was readying copy and sending it to be laid out. I figured they already had pow-wowed about the importance of each story.

I watched them work from the doorway. Few words were spoken. I wanted to wander behind each and see what they were writing, but knew I would distract them. Instead I stood in the doorway and observed.

Biff came in behind me and tried to shoulder check me out of his way. He sat at his desk and snarled in my direction then started typing furiously.

The editor made his rounds before making final decisions on news for page one. He stopped to talk to Biff to see what police news erupted over the weekend to begin planning the stories for the front pages and those that would run on the inside pages.

"What's new?" The editor stopped behind Biff and started reading his screen.

"Nothing. I got nothing. Thanks to Mr. Ace Reporter there," he pointed at me. "The police have shut us down. I couldn't even get past the front desk."

The editor turned to me. I thought his name was Chuck. "Can we interview you?"

Crap. What to do? I knew Clive would have a coronary if I gave up details about the case but then again, I was supposed to be teaching good interview techniques.

"My attorney wouldn't advise me to answer questions, but what if I write a story about my experience as a murder suspect?"

"I like it. Do it in thirty. Take Biff's desk. He's got nothing." The editor retreated to his office after the pronouncement.

I could feel the anger pulsing from Biff who had been blasted in front of his peers. I wasn't winning any friends with the editor's tactics and made at least one enemy. Most editors were snarling tigers looking to unleash their wrath on anyone close. No one was safe. Rule by fear. It worked in most newsrooms.

Biff chucked his notebook across the desk and rocketed himself back on the chair's wheels. I took a step forward but wasn't stupid enough to get within reach. He stomped out of the office. I grabbed the seat and pulled it up to the computer.

When he exited, the collective took a breath in unison and resumed their attention to their screens. I started typing, not sure where to go with the story.

By Mitch Malone

The clicking of the cuffs, the clang of the jail door and the dull thud of the judge's gavel were never sounds that I thought would determine my destiny.

That changed Saturday when Flatville Police Department arrested me for the murder of Trudy Harrison. When I found out I was wanted for questioning, I turned myself in. I am innocent and have nothing to hide. I suffered an interrogation with my attorney, Clive Darrow, at my side.

When authorities finished with questioning, they placed me under arrest, the cuffs attached to my wrists and led me to the jail.

As a reporter for the *Grand River Journal*, I have often covered the arrest of many criminals but I can't describe my uncertainty when I felt the cold steel on my wrists. Being uneasy is one thing but after being fingerprinted and led to a cell, you realize you can't get out. That simple fact can change a man.

I've been in cells before but always with the knowledge that I could get out anytime I wanted. The gloomy spirit that comes when the door slams shut is indescribable.

Had I not known of my own innocence, the prospect of spending any time in the small cell is daunting. After a night of fitful sleep, a couple of hours of pondering my situation and boredom, police led me out of the jail and to the courthouse for my arraignment.

Again, I have been on the audience side of the courtroom many times but being at the defense table was a new experience. The judge loomed larger than from the gallery seats. Every word burned into my brain. The sneer of the prosecutor who believes I am a scumbag murderer made me want to scream my innocence. The judge, who questioned my integrity and whether I would flee if released, challenged all the respect I'd earned as a reporter.

My attorney argued my dedication to my career and zealous action to prove my innocence which convinced the judge to allow bail even though it was a murder charge.

I'm actively looking to earn my freedom and remove any doubt about my guilt. If you have any information, please contact me at the Flatville paper or contact my attorney. No bit of information is too small.

I did some editing and polishing but thought it a lovely story that said nothing but screamed my innocence. I emailed a copy to Clive to make sure I wasn't inadvertently tainting my case. His response made me want to chuckle.

"Don't ever get into a sparring match with a person who buys his ink by the barrel. This should make the prospective jurors more amenable to your innocence."

Biff re-entered the newsroom and I hastily exited out of all programs and left his desk.

I walked to the editor's office and nodded, letting him know my story was ready for editing. I kept walking and headed to the back of the paper by the presses. I wanted some fresh air without animosity.

"Sorry about your arrest."

I turned and saw Scoop. Her coveralls dotted with black ink in a Rorschach test that would stump any psychiatrist. The first sympathy I'd gotten and I wanted to fall apart. This could not happen to Mitch Malone, decorated crime beat reporter, a hardened newspaperman. I nodded. "Thanks."

I could only manage the one word without showing how on edge I felt.

As if sensing my fragile condition, she turned back to the press and started threading newsprint through the big rollers.

"I thought you only used this press for small ads and such?"

"Usually we do, but today we are running an extra edition all about the murder. We'll sell it at businesses before the regular edition. It'll be great for the bottom line."

I nodded. My ass in jail would help this small rag make its budget projections. Something about this wasn't fair.

"Need any help?"

I couldn't believe this slip of a girl was running this monster of a press. "No, I got it."

A gray-haired man came out the side door we used to get to the library which seemed like weeks ago. He carried the large, tin, flexible plates that would apply the ink to the paper. The plates were a mirror image of the page so when the ink was transferred it would be readable. Even with the mirror image I could recognize my face and body with my hands cuffed behind. Sam on one side and the sheriff on the other. Any time elected officials could get their mug in the paper would make it easier to win election the next time around and keep their job. Nothing sinister about it, just good business for politicians. Mayor Ram Malone hadn't made it but then again he wouldn't want the world to know his cousin was arrested for murder.

I glanced closer to see if the shin kicks showed. Nothing in this photo. My good luck from poker was gone. It became worse when I looked at my face showing me made mad enough to kill. That wouldn't go over well with the jury. I hoped it wouldn't go to a jury.

Scoop caught me looking at the page and stopped to examine it as well.

"Not exactly your best side." She half-smiled at her joke.

"No, but not the best of circumstances either. Wish I hadn't been scowling."

"Mmmmm." Scoop leaned in to get a better view. "I wonder…" Without another word she turned on her heel and retreated the way she came. I didn't want to delay the printing even if it told of my unsubstantiated criminal inclination.

I wandered back toward the front. The team should be off deadline. I needed to see if the editor wanted any changes to my story. I doubted he would with my writing skills but needed to show courtesy and respect to his position and authority. You just had to kiss ass sometimes to make life easier. I'd learned that the hard way.

Biff returned to his desk and scowled as I entered. No one looked off deadline. Everyone still typed, intent on their copy, except the police reporter, who looked ready to kill. I only gave Biff a cursory thought as a real suspect although he drank a brew at the pub. I wandered back out again and took a seat in the lobby on a chair that looked older than I. The receptionist and classified ad person looked up, a question in her eyes. I shook my head and leaned back into the metal chair with thin emerald green plastic stretched over the seat and back.

I closed my eyes and tried to think about what I was going to say in the afternoon. I needed to stress there would be no discussion of the murder or charges against me . Knowing Biff, he would print anything I said.

The chair vibrated and I opened my eyes to see the lights return to brightness. I must have looked alarmed but the receptionist smiled at the lights. "The press started rolling." She returned her attention to her computer screen.

I returned to my pondering pose of moments ago. I tuned out the world when I was again wakened by a rude shout.

"Extra, Extra, read all about it." Scoop stood in front of me with newspapers draped over her arm.

"I thought you might like to read the first copies, hot off the press." She winked at me and her voice softened. She gave me the entire stack. "For your personal archives."

Scoop could be a smart ass when she wanted but I thought it sweet of her to personally deliver the edition to me first. She saluted and returned in the direction of the press using the side hallway away from the newsroom.

I opened the special edition and started reading. My piece, one from Biff detailing my arrest and another one from Bob with my arraignment comprised the front page along with Trudy as the pillar of the community and society matron. Her photo was the senior picture from the morgue.

As luck would have it, my photo was below the fold and not as noticeable compared to the giant headlines on the top. The paper rattled as I pulled it closer. I couldn't believe my eyes. My scowl vanished replaced by a flattened mouth that showed little emotion.

How had that happened?

I picked up my stack of papers and took them to the back and the noise of the press stopped me. I would never be able to ask and I couldn't see Scoop anywhere.

I started to turn when I saw her pop out from the back way to the front. I waved the paper at her and she gave me a thumbs-up sign.

I headed in her direction but she went to examine the press that spewed copies stacking them in neat bundles. Everything met to her satisfaction and she pointed toward the back hall.

As soon as the door closed, the noise lessened to a dull background buzz.

"What's up?" Scoop put her hands in her back pockets and rocked back on her heels.

"My picture? This wasn't the same one I saw on the plate? It couldn't have been changed that quickly could it?"

"The plate, no." A wide grin spread across.

"Well, spill." I put my hands to my hips to simulate a parental stance but the stack of papers I held threatened to spill.

She laughed. "Every now and then you get a bad spot on a plate and have to adjust it. I just took off a little around your mouth. I thought it looked rather good myself."

I laughed too. "You doctored the plate for me? Thank you but I'm not sure you should have. What if someone finds out?"

Scoop shrugged her shoulders. "So. It's not like they can fire me. I was never hired. Don't sweat it." With that she waved and returned out the door to the press.

I wandered toward the front and entered the conference room. Today's session would prove my point about going the extra mile. I placed a copy of the special edition at each chair. It would be a perfect exhibit for the newsroom that was putting me on trial in the media.

My stomach rumbled letting me know it was time for lunch. It could be my last meal before the firing squad in the conference room beginning promptly at one.

I headed toward the front intent on grabbing some fast food or doughnuts to silence my belly grumble, but instead ran into the publisher, Scoop's dad, and the advertising director headed out the door.

"Mitch, want to join us for lunch?" Montgomery Bradshaw's voice was cultured with a bit of a twang that years of living in the north hadn't beaten out yet.

"Thank you. I was headed out to pick something up before this afternoon's session. I might have to leave early to get back." I didn't want to spend my lunch dodging innuendo and not-too-subtle probing.

"Don't worry about that. They'll wait. I want to sit in on this afternoon's session as well. I might have to duck out on occasion but thought it something we all could use as a refresher course."

Great, not only would I be volleying shots from Biff and Bob but would now need to impress the publisher as well. I wasn't catching any breaks.

Chapter 18

EIGHT PEOPLE FILED in looking ready for a nap. Biff and Bob, the editor, publisher, two women I had seen in the newsroom that did features, the sports writer who had not been around Friday, all wandered in looking bored. Last in was Scoop who flashed me a quick thumbs-up sign. I saw her father give her a look and she smiled, almost saintly.

They took seats according to their pecking order. The publisher and editor closest to me. Biff and Bob on the far side nearly to the end and the woman on the opposite side with a chair between them. Scoop took a seat nearest me and the sports editor who looked barely old enough to shave sat next to her. He looked smitten when he smiled shyly at Scoop.

"I've placed in front of you today's special edition. I would like you to take a minute and look at the stories."

"Like we didn't write them." Biff snickered loud enough for all to hear.

I wondered if the publisher would curtail the heckling. I banked on no. I gave them a few moments to accomplish the task.

"What makes these pages different from the normal front page?" I looked around but didn't expect many comments.

"We have a murder. First time in I don't know how many years," the publisher said.

A snicker quickly became a cough.

"Yes, but what else. Look deeper," I prodded.

"You have a byline on our front page." Biff looked angelic.

I wanted to smack him. This wasn't about me but making the paper better, allowing it to survive in a downward economy that was going paperless. "Yes, but what else?"

Scoop looked up. Her eyes sparkled. "The stories are interesting and cover all aspects of the murder."

I smiled at her. "Yes, now you're on to something. What else?"

Biff and Bob looked at the paper in earnest trying to come up with something. They refused to let a high schooler one up them in front of the bosses. About time.

Biff looked up. "The stories are in depth." His voice was almost awed.

"Yes. That's correct, but what makes these more interesting than the ones that were done yesterday? Other than they deal with murder?" Now we were getting somewhere.

"We tried harder. With so many stories about one event, we had to work harder so they all had a distinct focus. Then we had to work harder to get comments from different people." I could see that Biff wanted to make light of it but couldn't.

"Yes."

"These weren't single source stories. Each one had at least three people quoted." The editor made his contribution talking slowly trying to weigh the information.

"But we can't do this every day. We have to work with what the news gives us." Bob's voice held a whiney edge.

"Can't you?" I challenged.

"No." Bob would not release my gaze, ready to fight for lazy journalism.

"Why not?" I volleyed back. This would determine whether my seminars would be a success or a failure. I had to come out on top. "Maybe you aren't looking at the stories in the right way."

"What way is that? Should I be arrested for the crime to get a good story?" He snickered until he realized no one else was laughing with him.

I ignored his dig. "What you need to think about is more of how can I get the complete picture in my stories? Have I exhausted all possible sources? Am I giving up on contacting a source?"

I pulled out an edition from last Tuesday that I had grabbed at random.

"Remember this edition? No murders here. What do we have?" I read the headlines: "City Council approves more patrol hours for officers. County administrator warns commission about budget deficits. Cat scrambles fire department. Elderly man recovers wallet."

I gave them a few moments to recall the stories.

"Let's start at the bottom of the page. The elderly man story is only three paragraphs. It doesn't contain any quotes and only attributes information to police sources. Why did this make the front page?"

"It was a human-interest piece," the editor responded.

"Where is the humanness or the interest?" I read the three paragraphs and saw Bob's ears turn red.

"What would have made this story more interesting?"

"Talking to the man whose wallet was returned," Scoop jumped in, happy to tromp on her nemesis.

"Speaking to the woman who found the wallet and getting quotes on why she returned it." This from Biff who looked like he wanted to distance himself from Bob.

"Better. Then add to that a quote from the cop who handled the report about how rare an occurrence that is." I paused for a moment to let my words sink in before I hit them with the clincher.

"If all three of those pieces would have been there, people on the street would have been talking about that story. The victim's family would have purchased newspaper copies and handed them out to friends. Who knows, next it could have been linked to a Facebook message or tweeted on Twitter."

I added the new technology references because of the publisher's presence. The newspaper was not leading the charge on going electronic. If it did, it would create additional revenues and larger readership.

We discussed what could have been done to each of the other stories until we worked to the top story, which was about the city council and the police department. I wanted more information about Sam's control. Good reporters use ulterior methods to attain information without anyone realizing their motives. I followed my own expert advice well.

"This piece had a good range of quotes from the city council, who discussed the issue at length. The heat of the comments shows through in the quotes." The editor sounded pleased with his assessment.

"Yes," I nodded in his direction. "How often is the city council at odds with the police department?"

Everyone looked to Biff who had written the story and was responsible for the city beat as well as crime. At small newspapers reporters covered multiple beats.

He shrugged his shoulders. "Not usually, but seems to be happening more and more. A couple city council members are questioning all expenditures for the police department."

"Why is that?" I probed.

"I'm not sure. Three members were new after the last election and they are trying to understand the budget process." Biff scratched his head.

"Have you asked them why they didn't like the expenditure?" It was a standard question.

"No, because they stated their reasons at the meeting." Biff was getting a little defensive and I didn't want to alienate him before I got the information I wanted.

"I don't mean for this story but it might be worth meeting them for coffee and getting to know them better so you can see if there is more to this than meets the eye. They might give you information on an even better story."

"When do you fit that in?" Biff's voice curious, not confrontational.

"You have to eat, don't you? Make them working lunches. Go to different places to eat and see who meets with whom. That might tell you who is cooking up the next big story." I had them now. I could feel their attention.

"Have you run any stories about a new recreational business along the river? A developer has already purchased the property and people are talking about it." I could see from their faces that this was news to their ears. "You have to become a member of the community you're covering."

"How do you do that?" Bob whined again. This guy was a seriously unhappy dude that I would like to drop kick out of the meeting.

"That's what being a reporter is all about—getting to know your sources. Find out if they have kids and what ages. You ask them about their children and then steer the conversation to what you want to talk about. That will be tomorrow's topic – interviewing techniques."

I looked at my watch, astounded that it was after four. "That's about it for today. See you tomorrow."

Montgomery or Monty as he asked me to call him over lunch stood and as if on cue, everyone rose and filed out. Glad to be released from their afternoon "in school."

"Thanks, Mitch. You got them thinking about their job. That is exactly what I needed. I knew you would be a good teacher, it's in your blood. After I got used to the idea of you coming and thought about it, I realized this would be good for the staff. I wouldn't take no for an answer."

He sounded so pompous and even puffed out his chest.

"Your editor tried to talk me out of it but it was because he didn't want you gone for a week. The circulation will suffer without your byline."

He still pumped my hand and I reeled from all the information. Teaching in my blood? Demanding I come here? "Thank you, sir," I muttered. I needed to get my interview skills out and see what he knew. "What made you think I would be a good teacher?"

"I knew your parents. Your father was a fine teacher. When he had something to say on the school board, people would naturally hush. He had an orator's voice."

"I never knew." I was reaching back into my past and not sure if I wanted to hear more or not.

Monty pulled his hand back and would have turned to go but with that little tidbit, I wanted more. I had forgotten so much about my parents. I remembered their anger and disappointment when I chose journalism and not education for my career path. Then they had died. End of discussion.

"Sir, would you mind telling me more about my parents?" My voice hesitant and unfamiliar to my own ears.

The publisher turned back and looked at me. I noticed Scoop behind him for the first time.

"How about if Mitch, err, Mr. Malone comes for dinner? Monday is meatloaf night but we could always order pizza instead." Her voice grew cajoling on the end as if she would prefer the pizza to the meatloaf. Me, the meatloaf sounded grand over my usual restaurant diet.

"Well, I guess that would be okay. Yeah, sure. Mitch we would love to have you for dinner."

"Thank you, sir. I look forward to it. What time?"

"Why don't you come with me now?" Scoop's voice was excited.

"Sarah, that isn't necessary. I'm sure Mitch wants to go change into more relaxed attire." Monty looked at what I was wearing and only frowned slightly when he saw my jeans. The only thing I would have to remove to be more casual was my tie.

"Our dining is rather casual during the week." The publisher explained. "Why don't we say six?"

"Could I bring anything?" I amazed myself. I did have manners and knew the proper protocol.

"No need." He nodded in my direction and I knew I was being dismissed as he exited the room.

I loosened my tie and unbuttoned the top button of my shirt. Did my tie and blazer have anything to do with my sudden formal manners? My parents drummed Ms. Manners' maxims into me for years and now they naturally flowed out. I wasn't sure if it was the town, the publisher's formal cadence or my mother's ghost whispering in my head. Flatville was changing me and I wasn't sure it was a direction I wanted to go. I also knew with this first trickle of information, that I wanted the dam to break to find out everything I'd forgotten. I felt the void their deaths had left and felt driven to fill it.

I hadn't given any serious thought to my parents in years and here I was begging for a dinner invitation to hear more. I'd forgotten my dad attended the meetings on the second and fourth Mondays trying to improve public education. He was all about broadening minds no matter what age. They believed everything should be a teaching lesson. I didn't believe any of that philosophy had rubbed off but now I recognized I channeled some of my father and his lectures during my presentation.

I wished I had paid more attention to what had happened when they'd died. I was in a daze and so angry. I had been named editor of the university's newspaper and afraid I would lose the position if I spent more than a day or two in Flatville. Uncle Rich had volunteered to handle it and I'd let him. They had a will and Judge Roosevelt had handled the probating. I'd received a check from Uncle Rich that I used to place the down payment on my condo.

I'd never thought about that being the sum total of their life on earth. A check. What would be left if I left this earth soon? I didn't have a will. I didn't even have someone to leave the money to.

I couldn't think about that now. I had to exonerate myself from a murder charge, but I also yearned for more about my parents. The best way I could accomplish both was by being a reporter and asking questions. I would start tonight with the publisher. Pick his brain. Next on my list would be Harold.

Who else should be on my list? Ram's dad, Richard Senior, had been close to my dad. They'd been brothers. I hadn't thought about that connection until he stepped forward to pay my bail. Not that I was looking forward to seeing Ram, but I'd never thought about having an uncle to look out for me. I wasn't sure I would be in Flatville long enough to ever look forward to that visit.

Chapter 19

"SO YOU KNEW my parents?" The question popped before I had a chance to think it through. At least I'd waited until everyone's plate was filled and a few pleasantries exchanged.

Monty nearly spit his first bite of meatloaf onto the table. I wasn't sure if it was burning his mouth or my question caught him off guard. Scoop tried not to laugh.

"Well, yes." He brought up his cloth napkin and dabbed at his lips and took a hasty swallow of his bourbon and water he'd brought to the table with him. His Adam's apple bobbed with the effort.

"At that time I covered the school board." He stopped and cleared his throat making it a deeper timbre as if he was getting ready to launch into a sermon. "Your father was president and he ran a tight meeting. Prior to his term, meetings lasted until eleven o'clock. During his tenure they were never longer than an hour and a half."

Great, he could run a meeting but what did that tell me about the person I never knew.

"Your father had a great sense of humor. He cracked jokes when things got tense especially around teacher contract time."

"Daaaad." Scoop drew out the name as if in exasperation.

The publisher looked at Scoop, surprised to see her. "Mitch wants to know the things like I ask about mother." Scoop was more intuitive than I thought. She would make a great reporter.

"Oh, yes. I see. Let me think." Silence stretched as he thought about what to say in a more personal vein. "I know you were their pride and joy.

After the meetings when I would ask the reasoning behind his position, he often said: 'I have a son who goes to school here and I base my decision on what I would want for him.'"

"What were important issues for him?"

His forefinger came up and stroked his cheek. "Well, that is hard to say. He championed any program that helped kids who needed a little extra with their education. He started the first mentor tutoring program. Strong-armed several business people to come into the elementary and read with or read to those who weren't reading up to grade level." The publisher chuckled and I wanted to know the joke.

"I remember all the grumbling from business owners saying they didn't have time for that. Your dad challenged them. Said give it two months and if they wanted to quit, they could and he wouldn't ask again. You know, not a single one quit and many of them still do it today. I did a follow-up story after the two months and every one of them said how much they got out of the program and didn't know if it benefited the kids or not."

"Did it?" I was a sponge and wanted every bit of information.

"Yes. A year later test scores increased by ten percent and every kid who had a mentor was reading at or beyond grade level by the following year. Those were some results." He paused and I wanted to prod for more but I didn't have to.

"The governor wanted him to come to Lansing and receive an award for being a friend of education. He refused unless the governor convened the state school board to hear a presentation on the program. The governor did and now mentoring programs are common in the majority of the school systems in the state."

Again the publisher chuckled. "I wrote a great feature on your father and the photos were inspired. We had a photo of your dad in a little seat with his knees to his chin reading to a student. Then we ran a photo of him lecturing the school board. That article, but mostly the photos garnered a Michigan Press Association Award that year."

"It was a loss to the community when your parents were killed. A real shame. They could have used him when they were building the new high school. Your father opposed purchasing the property south of town without an environmental study about contaminants. That issue split the community right down the middle. Some didn't want to waste money on an expensive study, they wanted to get the school built." Monty trailed off for a minute deep in thought.

I looked down at my plate and hadn't touched a bite. I scooped up a piece of meatloaf. It was moist and tasty. I kept glancing at him waiting for him to finish.

"You were saying, sir?" I hoped that pushed whatever he thought about into words.

"Mitch, your talk today got me thinking about that old story. I didn't ask enough questions. Your dad was so adamant, people were willing to have the study to get the project moving. Then he was killed in that accident. No one ever mentioned the study again. Turned out the land was contaminated and the school district spent thousands of dollars on clean up that could have been spent on education. I wonder…"

The publisher took a couple of bites and conversation dipped at the table as he was thinking about his memories. I wanted him to share more but didn't want to push too much.

"So Scoop, any idea where you want to go to college?" I was making conversation and wanted to treat her like a grown up.

"I'm thinking Central Michigan because they have a great journalism program there."

I saw the publisher turn red. "Sarah, both your mother and I were University of Michigan graduates and planned on you following the tradition." The sentence was said in a light voice but there was steel behind the words.

"I know, Dad, but I wouldn't be able to even write for the school paper until I was a junior. At Central I can get on right away."

"What about your business degree?" His tone curt, brooking no argument.

"Dad, I don't want a business degree. I want to write," she wailed.

"Sarah, we will discuss this later, not in front of our guest."

The discussion was over and I remembered similar ones in my home about getting a journalism degree. I made a mental note to lobby for Scoop at a later date. Now to move the conversation back to what I wanted to know.

"What about my mother?"

"I didn't know her well. I remember your father saying that she was in line to become president of West Central University. I'm not sure if that was wishful thinking or not. The university back then never had a female president or vice president. When she died I think there was talk about her almost being named a vice president but I don't know for sure. The university was never any place I covered."

He thought for a moment. "My wife knew her better and that is where I might have gotten that information. My wife was very woman's lib back then and was pleased about the appointment. She wanted to do a story on the first woman vice president and make a big deal out of it and then your mother died and I never heard anything about it. My own wife died shortly after that. So many memories that I never thought about the timing of things."

Another quiet lapse of conversation while we all shoveled in our food. We'd had enough talk and now I wanted to get out. There was so much I wanted to check into and had never thought about. Tomorrow I would be at the paper bright and early reading the old articles about my parents.

Chapter 20

I WOKE TENSE and edgy trying to stretch my tight muscles hoping to relax. Sleep had been filled with strange dreams I couldn't remember. Every family photo I could remember was swirled around in a strange vortex reminiscent of Alice's trip down the Wonderland hole.

The window illuminated no light but the clock glowed six-thirty. I showered and dressed and went through the kitchen, snatching three pieces of coffee cake for breakfast.

It was early and much of the newspaper was dark. I sat at the morgue computer but Scoop had pulled out the stories. I wasn't sure where to start. What would I find? Why did I want to know? Flatville was never a happy place for me and coming back was a bad idea. I started to turn on the computer but stopped. Anything on my parents would still be in the file cabinets.

"Touch that switch and prepare to lose your fingers." The voice as severe as the hair pulled back into a bun. "What are you doing in my library?" She tapped the sign on the door. "No admittance without permission," it read.

"Sorry. Scoop showed it to me over the weekend."

"Scoop's got special permission. You do not." Her voice was stern at the end. "Who are you?"

"Mitch Malone. I'm doing seminars. I'm on loan you could say." I gave a self deprecating smile to try and soften her up. "From the *Grand River Journal*."

"This isn't a self-service operation. No one messes with my system. What are you looking for?"

"I used to live here and was looking for some stories." I paused trying to put into words what I wanted but I wasn't sure. "Do you have a file on Timothy Malone?"

She looked at me narrowing her eyes trying to make a decision. "These clips aren't for anyone off the street."

"I know. I just…" I stopped. I could go to the library and read back issues but they wouldn't be sorted by name. It would take longer than a week. The dragon turned her back and I felt like I was dismissed. I didn't want to search. I wanted the file handed to me. I was Mitch Malone, ace sleuth and seminar presenter extraordinaire. At my morgue I was given allowances and special treatment. I wasn't in Grand River anymore and wanted to throw something to vent my frustration. I felt alone and beaten by the town that had welcomed my birth.

I headed to the door and vowed to have Scoop come back with me after hours, but I didn't want to wait that long. Now that the door had been opened to my past I wanted information.

"Why don't you sit here and look at the file?"

Her words didn't sink in at first. I looked at her and she held a gold colored envelope.

"That way I can keep an eye on you and make sure the contents stay and in the same condition."

I was in kindergarten and agreeing to share the Crayolas. I wanted that file with a desperation I couldn't explain. My life was in that file or at least a part of it I hadn't thought about for a long time.

She placed the envelope in front of me after I returned to the seat. I hestitated only a few seconds for her to move away before I opened the flap, pulled out dozens of clips from a couple paragraphs to full-page spreads and started to read.

The stories piled into a chronological order and started with my father's graduation from Flatville High School, then college. Another named him as professor of psychology at West Central University in Flatville. A short wedding announcement complete with a photo of the happy couple. I stared at the photo for several minutes thinking about my childhood and their love for me and each other. Their death intruded along with the pain. Anger had been my motivating emotion during those days after. I hadn't wanted the house, its contents or anything from them. Now I wished I had at least taken a couple of photos.

After the funeral I never returned to Flatville. I didn't want any reminders. It all disappeared and I wasn't sure who did it or where it went. I pushed their death back like I had Aaron's. If I never thought about it, it wouldn't hurt. A flood of emotion started deep in my chest with a couple of small chinks, then a ripping. I pushed it back just like I had so long ago. It wouldn't go. The dam opened and the river now cascaded and escalated. The pain. The hurt. The emptiness. The regret. It raged to escape but I didn't know how to let it go. It started in my heart and moved through to my stomach upsetting my control like a tornado. I could not let this happen. Not here. Not now.

Damn. I left Flatville for a reason. I should not be here. A single tear leaked from my eye. Would that gain in momentum like the pain? The salty water rolled down my cheek before I wiped it away. I was Mitch Malone, hardnosed newspaper man, who did not get all misty-eyed from a wedding photo even if it showed my dead parents.

I took a deep breath and a box of Kleenex dropped down on the desk beside my elbow. I ignored it and the gesture. Kindness would not help me gain control. I turned the article over and went on to the next one. A paragraph on my birth. That one went into the read pile.

After that, the school board election dominated including my father's platform. Issues he was adamant about, programs he wanted to see implemented and then about ten years after I was born, the feature by Mr. Bradshaw. It took the top two-thirds of the page and featured the photos. I remembered this man who spouted principles about the value of education at the dinner table, trying to drum academia into my brain when my interests involved playing baseball or riding my bike.

The classics I'd read like *Tale of Two Cities*, *Tom Sawyer*, and *Animal Farm* bored me. They would then be discussed at the dinner table. If my answers didn't pass his approval, I wasn't allowed to go outside until I had successfully discussed the goals and motivations of the characters. It was torture.

I shook my head trying to clear those days that I thought were so horrible and didn't seem quite so bad now. I moved to the next clip. More school board stories. My eyes felt heavy and gritty, my shoulders sagging forward, but I kept slogging through them realizing my dad had had a large impact on Flatville's schools.

As I neared the end I realized the frequency increased in the articles. Mostly the stories came out after the twice-a-month meetings but this batch was a couple a week. I stopped and paged back and started reading from the beginning of the issue that sparked so much debate.

The school board was discussing locations for a new high school. My father lobbied for land within the community and two others on the board wanted to put the school in a field five miles from town.

The location seemed to be discussed at every meeting. A local real estate agent presented land values and survey results from surrounding districts and the locations of their high school.

The discussion went on for months. A couple of times the stories mentioned Richard A. Malone, Sr. lobbying for the out of town location citing decreased vandalism from kids walking to school and back home again and keeping the kids out of the downtown where they scared the customers. I did remember my father mentioning the debate the last time I was home for Christmas break, but hadn't paid any attention—another boring educational lecture. Now I wished I'd listened.

Why had he been so passionate about it? Why did he care? It was only a high school's location, not the theory of relativity.

I read more concentrating on my father's quotes. He was against the location but the stories weren't balanced. My father's quotes were only tokens. If I ran the paper, I would be yanking that reporter off the story. Then I berated myself for standing up for my dad now that it was too late.

I went back and looked at the bylines of the stories. Montgomery Bradshaw. This kind of reporting explained why the newspaper needed my help now. Monty could write a decent feature but his news sense seemed a bit off.

Maybe past issues will be today's topic at the seminar and see what pops out.

Did it matter? My parents were dead. Their issues were long gone headlines. Issues settled. Move on, Malone, I commanded.

But I couldn't. I kept reading about the debate of the school location.

My father's tidbits in the paper seemed logical and never answered except with rhetoric with the other school board members.

I flipped to the next page and stopped. I wasn't ready for this. How can someone go from arguing for a school location to dead in the next breath? But he had. His obituary. My eyes blurred. He had died so long ago. Why was I tearing up now? I should be over it. I was tired. I had a murder charge hanging over my head. It was a reaction to the stress of giving the seminars and facing a murder rap. That was it. I willed the tears back in much the same way I had done at the actual funeral. I'd been stoic, in shock and didn't remember much of it except for the gleaming coffin. I wondered whose job it was to buff it up so it nearly glowed in the muted light of St. Michael's Catholic Church. The strange things you remember like the two caskets in front of the altar, brass handles gleaming. The white cloth that symbolized their freedom from earthly sin shrouded the caskets. I wore the suit my parents had given for Christmas to wear for job interviews now called into duty. I never wore it again. I'd left it behind when I returned to college. Details kept flooding back, unbidden and unwanted. I refused to remember more and returned to the clips. I'd tried to forget it all.

I turned the obituary over with more force, only a few more. The final clipping described the next school board meeting and several subjects. Only six inches of discussion debated the naming of the new school as a tribute to my father for his eighteen-plus years of dedication to the school board. This one Monty nailed with balance and sincerity now that my father was dead.

Uncle Rich had a quote about the Malone name having a long tradition of service in the community and a fitting tribute making sure to mention the hardware store as well.

My dad's most vocal opponent, a Fred Smith, seemed to be a colorful character. "Tim Malone didn't want this high school, at least not in its current location. He sure as tootin' wouldn't want his name on it."

I had to chuckle at that because it was true. My dad would never want his name on a building. That thought brought back a flood of memories of the discussion of naming buildings at the university after whoever had given the most money. Donors would compete against themselves to be able to have a building named after them. My dad thought the process a disservice and would come back to bite the university. My parents would laugh when donors with more money than sense would appear in the paper. The school nearly named a prestigious building on campus after a CEO of a dotcom business that tanked from embezzlement.

I put the articles back in the envelope and handed them to the dragon. "Could I see…" I stopped. What did I want? I needed information. I needed to stop thinking like a crybaby and more like the reporter I had been since leaving Flatville. What did I know other than I was going to be tried for murder of Trudy Harrison? Trudy was upset about what had happened to Aaron. I needed to look at Aaron.

That was another bloody wound I had pushed aside. If I could do it with my parents, I could do it with Aaron. I stood and caught the dragon's attention.

"Could I see the file for Aaron Oppenhizen?" I waited for an argument but was relieved with her silent compliance.

She left on her task and pulled out a small envelope.

I walked back to the desk and set it down and then attempted to get comfortable in the old office chair. I pulled myself in, then pushed myself back. Each time the chair squawked in protest.

I couldn't delay. Time to face my demons. I opened the envelope. Three stories fluttered out.

The first story outlined sketchy details about the accident. A boy's body found in the Green River in the national forest. Authorities not releasing the name of the victim until next of kin notified. Warnings from the police about jumping into the river without checking the depth first, typical stuff I'd used to pad my stories when sources refused to talk.

The next story was the longest. It quoted the high school principal, Aaron's homeroom teacher, his neighbors. Talked about what a great young man he'd been. How shocked they were. It also gave all the funeral information. The last article was about the funeral. It quoted the minister and had a brief statement from the family. It showed his ninth grade photo with the hair looking greasy because we'd wetted it down so his cowlick didn't look like Alfalfa from the "Little Rascals."

Done. Aaron's life in three short stories. No one had said he was the best third baseman Flatville had ever seen. That he was loyal to a fault. I had to stop at this point and suck in air to keep my emotions in check. I wanted to throw something, kick the trash can or make a big sweep across the desk pushing anything in my path to a heap on the floor. I wanted to damage something in the hopes it would heal the wound that gapped in my chest where my cold heart felt the heat of emotion.

"This building is so dusty. Makes one's allergies kick up. Lots of runny noses." She was giving me an easy out if I wanted to use a tissue. I was a tough reporter. I didn't cry. I investigated. I looked back at the stories. One thing stood out. Nowhere was there any information on why he had died. I assumed that had been left out to not cause the family any additional trauma.

I'd made decisions like that in my stories. Sometimes the public's right to every gaudy detail didn't justify printing every aspect. At times it also got me a great follow-up with the parents who appreciated my delicacy. Maybe the paper's policy was not to mention the cause of deaths. No one had give one for Trudy either but her death was different. It had been murder. My parents and Aaron only tragic accidents.

I put the articles back in the envelope and rose from the computer. The Dragon met me at the door and I handed her the envelope. She handed me one in return. I took a quick look. It contained photo copies of the clips from my dad's file.

"You come back any time you need anything, Mr. Malone."

"Thank you." I left stunned by her thoughtfulness which put my frayed nerves to the surface. I was halfway to the press room when I looked at my watch and realized it was nearly noon and my seminar only an hour away.

Chapter 21

I DISMISSED THE seminar participants for a short afternoon break. I'd needed some fresh air and had walked back to the press room and snagged a candy bar and Coke out of the machines. Today was going well despite my emotional rollercoaster this morning.

"Mr. Malone," the front receptionist said from the door leading to the lobby. "Scott Nicewander is here to see you."

I took a step back from the lobby door to ensure I couldn't be seem by him and forced to take the meeting. I couldn't face the third Muskateer. I'd already nearly cracked when I read three clips about Aaron's death. I panicked. "Tell him, tell him I'm unavailable."

I entered the seminar room and put Scott out of my mind. The remaining hour and half flew by and we finished up around four-thirty. I figured the staff could either leave a few minutes early or still have time to return some phone calls.

I was the last to leave and was turning out the lights.

"Mr. Malone."

I turned and the receptionist was there again. Scott wouldn't have waited two hours to see me would he? He wanted to carry the reunion a little far. "Please, call me Mitch if we are going to keep meeting like this."

She didn't seem amused and handed me two pink squares of paper with messages and a *Flatville Gazette* envelope sealed with my name on the front in blocked capital letters with two heavy lines underneath to accent the name.

I glanced at the two messages. One from Clive asking for a return call and another from Harold telling me dinner was at six if I wanted to join them. I pushed the envelope into my back pocket behind my notebook and returned to the conference room to use the phone to call Clive.

Clive picked up on the first ring.

"It's Mitch. What's up?"

"Just received notice that your preliminary hearing will be Friday."

"So soon? I know they have to do it within 14 days but within a week is quick." My palms had begun to sweat and the receiver slipped.

"I figure they've gotten the reports back and feel they have enough to bind you to circuit court for trial. Remember the prosecution only has to prove that a crime was committed and evidence supports that you did it."

"Yes but what could they have other than I took her to breakfast? The autopsy has to show she was killed after I dropped her off?" My voice raised an octave and I tried to swallow but my mouth was like a desert.

"I've requested copies of all the reports and they will be delivered by nine tomorrow. Can we meet to go over them?"

"Sure. I don't need to be at the paper until one. I'll see you then."

I hung up and sat in the darkening room. The sun had disappeared between a batch of cumulus clouds. I could be back in jail by Friday evening if something or someone didn't get fingered for the crime. The cops were looking only at me as a suspect. No need to look elsewhere. They thought I did it and Sam was reinforcing their determination.

Who could have killed Trudy? I couldn't answer that because I didn't even know Trudy. Could Ram, my cousin, have killed her? I didn't like Ram. He had been a bully since he was two but that was a far cry from murder. Or was it just next in a progression of violence?

If I were approaching this as a reporter, I would go visit Trudy's parents and find out what she was like. Would they throw me out if I showed up? Couldn't hurt to try. I'd been thrown out before. That was all part of the being a reporter. You had to ask. I'd been telling that to the reporters in my seminar. I needed to follow my own advice.

I called Harold and thanked him for the dinner invitation, but I had other plans.

I pulled up in front of the Harrison house and the envelope in my back pocket grabbed as I exited. I pulled it out and tossed it on the passenger seat. Her home was a basic brick ranch that didn't look like it had changed in twenty years. Pink petunias lined the walk and I wondered if Trudy had encouraged their growth.

I rang the bell and heard some shuffling inside. The door opened and the interior was dim. Trudy's father looked unkempt. He was still wearing maroon-striped pajamas with stains from a meal that I didn't want to dissect. A lot of straight white hair hung down over his forehead. It looked like he was taking Trudy's death hard.

He scooped the fallen locks back as he looked up squinting into the early evening sunlight at my taller frame. The clouds having been chased away by a stiff breeze.

"You want something, feller?"

"Hi." I paused and decided not to use my name. "I'm from the *Flatville Gazette* and I would like to talk to you about your daughter."

"She's gone." He started to shut the door.

I thought that an odd statement to make about a woman who had died only four days ago. "I want to talk about her, not to her."

"Oh." I could see him puzzling that out. He must have decided I was alright and he turned around heading back into the dim interior.

I followed, taking time to shut the door behind me.

We entered a living room filled with clutter. Photos of Trudy were everywhere from baby pictures through high school, like a shrine. I expected to see her cheerleading uniform mounted behind Plexiglas on the wall.

While Trudy was everywhere, there were only a few photos of the family unit. One was apparently taken on vacation in the south with palm trees and another was in front of a green car that reminded me of one I wished for as a youth. I was surprised to realize I'd forgotten Trudy had a younger brother, Kim. I remember thinking as a kid that I wasn't fond of the name Mitch but glad my parents hadn't given me a girl name. He must have been several years younger than Trudy. A surprise as they called an unexpected pregnancy back then.

I looked again at the wall of photos, mostly just Trudy. The old gent shuffled to an oversized armchair that had seen better days. Next to it was a side table with a lamp and piled on it was a variety of dirty plates, cups and glasses. If I had to guess, I'd say a couple of day's worth. I wasn't the best at keeping my place clean but at least I threw out the paper plates before they started to mold.

The guy had suffered a terrible loss. I could forgive his lack of housekeeping in his grief.

"What you selling?"

I was startled by the voice and realized the man was seated in his chair, remote in hand although the TV was muted.

"Nothing. I'm not selling anything. I wanted to talk about Trudy." I perched on the sofa next to the table beside his chair. I could see the TV and it looked like a rerun of "I Love Lucy."

"Are you here to fix my TV? Can't get any sound out of it." He waved the remote in the direction of the picture.

"No, I wanted to talk about Trudy, your daughter."

"She ain't here. Don't know where she is. Should be coming home any time now from her job and getting my dinner."

Something wasn't right here. Hadn't anyone broken the news to him about his daughter being killed?

"When was the last time you saw her?" I leaned in.

He thought for a minute. "She came home upset and was prowling around the living room. She'd started crying. I asked her what was wrong, but she shook her head and told me to go back to bed. She'd handle it. Once and for all."

I could see pain behind his eyes. Maybe I had woken him and he'd forgotten and now the memories were flooding back. "Do you remember when that was?"

He was silent. A tear welled up and then dripped down his cheek.

"You here to fix the sound on my TV? I can't get it to work." He again waved the remote at the TV.

"No. I'm here about your daughter, Trudy."

"She ain't here. She should be home soon to get my dinner."

I felt like déjà vu. The moldy plates stank but so did the whole situation. Trudy's father needed help. Trudy lived her own version of the old Twilight Zone series when someone alters your family's mind.

I didn't want to listen to him rewind and begin again. Maybe I could rustle up something for him to eat. Open cereal boxes laid on their sides spilled across the kitchen counter. Coffee grounds sprinkled across aged-yellow linoleum. The flies feasted on dried liquids on the table and counter that I didn't want to identify.

No valuable information would come from her dad and if it did, I would never be sure of its veracity or exactly when in time it occurred. The strain I saw in Trudy now had a cause. It wasn't anything sinister, it was concern for her father's mental condition. That still didn't explain why she was murdered though.

What to do? Who to call?

I heard footsteps behind me. "Don't worry about the mess. Trudy will clean it up. She'll be along soon to cook my dinner."

I nodded. Where were the casseroles? Didn't people bring casseroles when someone in the family died? I remember our kitchen being filled with food when my parents had died. Had Flatville forgotten its duty?

"Are you here to fix to my TV? I can't get any sound out of the darn thing? Trudy always fixed it. Where is Trudy? She should be home soon."

I reached for the wall phone and dialed the only person I knew who could be of some help, then I hit the mute button on his remote. Lucille Ball's cackling laughter echoed off the walls. I sat down to wait. Her father returned to his chair and never said another word.

What would happen to him now? I shouldn't care or even worry but I had had a crush on Trudy all those years ago. I had to find Trudy's real killer. Someone had to pay and the price had gone up.

The doorbell rang and Trudy's father didn't move. Had he heard it over the sound of the TV? I opened the door a crack, then swung it wide to allow to allow Harold and Kate to enter. I took my time following, making sure I'd shut the door. I looked at all the photos on the walls as I returned to the living room.

Watching Trudy's dad pained me. I didn't want to see it again. What had happened here? When had Trudy's mother died? How long had Trudy been caring for him? Where was the brother? Why wasn't he taking care of his dad? I didn't even know where the brother lived. This explained why Trudy returned to Flatville even if she didn't want to. The sadness in her eyes must have been from reliving her happy teen years and then knowing she had to return to a father who may not recognize her. I would have been chugging the hard liquor too in her situation. I wish I'd known. I don't know what I could have done but at least Trudy would have had someone to talk to in her last hours. I could be a good listener. I wouldn't even have taken notes for a story.

When I returned down the hall, Harold had turned the TV's volume lower and sat where I had. He asked questions and Trudy's father answered. The clinking of plates and silverware could be heard coming from the kitchen.

"Trudy, we have guests. Could you make some coffee?" He looked toward the kitchen and I heard Harold ask another question.

I shook my head, chin resting on my chest. As I entered, the kitchen was a blaze of light as the overhead fluorescents showed the true extent of the disaster. The flies circled and buzzed the light interrupted from their feasting.

"Trudy will bring coffee out in a few minutes. She must have had to work late today." The words floated in from the living room.

I stopped and surveyed the scene, not sure what to do now. Warm arms snaked around my waist and propelled me to a kitchen chair pushing me into it. The arms again enveloped me from behind over my shoulders.

I'm not sure what came over me or how long we stayed like that. Tears rolled down my cheeks. I didn't know if I was crying for Trudy, her dad, my being charged, or the three deaths that drove me from Flatville so many years ago. I didn't make a sound but couldn't stop the liquid from leaking out of my eyes. Life wasn't fair and I was acting like a two-year-old who lost his favorite stuffed animal. I reached up and made hand-to-hand contact letting the warmth of Kate's bony fingers calm my over-active emotions. She made soothing noises and I leaned into her warm wrinkly arm, resting my head. I don't know how long we stayed like that but then my time was up. She patted my head.

"It will be alright Mitch, You'll see." Kate returned to the sink and started running hot water. I sat and watched her fill the drainer with clean plates, cups and silverware.

"Mitch, honey."

I looked up and she handed me a towel. I dried.

Chapter 22

I WENT BACK to the bar. I needed a beer. The Shoemakers had cleaned and scrubbed and then called a couple of neighbors. Trudy's father wouldn't be left alone any time soon and steps were being taken to assess his situation and see if he could stay in the home.

I'd taken a peek at Trudy's room and found it trashed and the window broken. I pulled out my camera and took photos. Had the police done this? Had whoever killed Trudy done this? I was surprised they hadn't trashed the entire house and maybe they had. Who could tell?

I sat at the bar. There was a different bartender working but he had his back to me talking into the phone. "I don't care if it is your night off. If you want to keep this job, you better get your ass in here. I've got to meet with some guys. It can't wait."

I thought about all the hassles of owning a business and knew it would never be for me. Uncle Rich and Ram ran the hardware store and seemed to have lots of time. Flatville still ran on the old school of thought. They closed every night at six and never opened on Sunday. I didn't know what, if any, hobbies Uncle Rich or Ram had.

It would take a lot to run a bar/restaurant like this. I felt bad for the guy having to threaten employees to come in. He turned and I recognized Kim Harrison, Trudy's brother.

"What'll you have?"

I nodded in the direction of the beer taps. "Draft." Was the reason he needed to leave to go home and take care of his father? Maybe that was why the house was in a mess. The sole caregiver now had a business to run and ailing father and he couldn't manage—two, twenty-four-hour-a-day jobs. I felt sorry for him until I remembered the confrontation he had with Trudy when I brought her home. Could he have killed his own sister in a fit of anger? She'd called him a drug addict. In a fit of withdrawal rage could he have come back after I left, argued or tried to take money from her by force? When she wouldn't hand it over, he had struck out at her causing her to fall and hit her head? Had the Shoemakers at my request came and cleaned up evidence of murder that could exonerate me? Had their father witnessed it and that had pushed him further into his illness by not wanting to face the loss of his daughter at his son's hands? So many things were starting to make sense.

Kim grabbed a frosted mug and set to filling the liquid on an angle to reduce the foam. He was good at his job. "You look rough." He set the brew in front of me.

I looked into the mirror behind the bar and realized it was true. I caught myself from running my hand through my hair. It was standing on end in parts from doing just that too often.

"Long day." I took a large swig of my beverage and the wet cold liquid soothed my throat. I didn't want to add that I'd been doing the job of caring for his father and making arrangements for him.

I placed a five on the bar for my beer. I wasn't planning on having another. We stared at each other for a few minutes and I wondered if we were both thinking the other could have killed Trudy. He broke the silence.

"You're that reporter dude, aren't you? You were with my sister?"

I nodded. "You and Trudy always argue like that?" As a reporter, I've found the most direct questions usually resulted in the best answers.

"We were never close. I was seven years behind her in school. I could never live up to Trudy in my parent's eyes. Trudy got all As. Trudy was the Homecoming Queen. Trudy married a big time lawyer." He stopped realizing he gave away too much.

"I know the feeling." Exchanging a bit of personal information always helped build the rapport and usually led to greater confidence. "I could never live up to my cousin, Ram either. Football quarterback, Homecoming King. You name it, Ram was tops in his class."

Kim chuckled. "When she came home and told my dad her marriage was over, I was secretly glad. It was the first time she ever failed at anything. Problem was she didn't return to the posh suburbs of Detroit. No, she moved in with dad. Even when she was screwing up, she was ruining my life. I just can't catch a break." Kim picked up a bar rag.

Good. I needed to keep him talking. Wish I could record it but it was too late for that. He was giving a good motive for wanting Trudy dead that could at least cast reasonable doubt on my case.

"Ram was cool. Trudy let me hang out with them sometimes. He would throw a football to me. I was glad when he started dating her and then I didn't get picked on." He wiped the counter collecting the condensation from my glass.

"That's another reason I hate my parents. Who would ever name their son Kim? It's a damn girl's name." He opened the rag flat on the bar and then folded it in half, then again.

I nodded totally understanding his gripe but hate was such a harsh word.

"My parents were always on my case to study harder, read more. I just wanted to be outside with my friends." I hated casting my parents as the bad guys in this but hoped they understood. They wanted me to succeed and I have. I thought they would be proud of me even though I wasn't a teacher.

"By the time I was born, mom and dad were so old, they couldn't do anything. My dad never played catch with me." Kim picked up the rag by the top corner unfurling it, then wiped up another section of the bar taking a step away from me.

"Ram's dad helped me too. I got to know him really well. That's why I bought this business. He told me all about what it's like to run the hardware store and I knew this was the perfect place for me." He stepped back and refolded the rag.

I nodded and realized this was my perfect opportunity. "Are there other places to eat?"

"Not as good as Main Street Pub." He said the words proudly.

He moved off down the bar and did a few dishes. I looked around and realized he had only six customers and was bored. It was early in the week. He disappeared behind a door and when he returned he carried two red plastic baskets with fries piled high and some type of burger. I caught a whiff and my stomach growled.

I'd turned down dinner with the Shoemakers to see Trudy's dad. Talk about a disaster. I wondered what was wrong with him but figured it was Alzheimer's or something. Why didn't anyone know? Had Trudy come back to take care of her father and never told anyone?

A juicy burger sounded good—always settled me. Hoped it worked today.

After Kim came back, I placed my order and he relayed it to the kitchen. Time to get him talking again. "You own the place?"

"Sure do. Was the bartender when old man Scroggins wanted to spend his winters in Florida. We worked out the arrangements and I ran it while he enjoyed the warmth. When he returned, he sold it to me and now it's mine."

"How's it going?"

"Good mostly. I enjoy tending the bar and I have a good staff. It works. I'm happy."

"That's all that counts."

A bell sounded somewhere and Kim turned to leave. He returned with a red basket and my mouth started to water. He placed it in front of me and I didn't wait for an invitation. I hefted the burger and took a bite.

"What do you think?" Kim pointed to my burger that was dripping with yellow, red and brown condiments.

I chewed slowly testing out the combination of flavors. I considered myself a burger connoisseur. I would travel miles out of my way if I knew a good burger joint was available. I'd done a little matchmaking for two people who had a particular love of burgers. They had their own place now up near the mighty Mackinaw Bridge, feeding tourists.

"Not bad. I've eaten burgers all over the state. I'd say this could be in the top twenty."

Kim frowned and got an ugly look in his eye. I looked over his physique and while he was still on the short side, his shoulders were well-developed. I was sure he had no problem tossing unruly patrons out the door, literally. I didn't want to be one of them, especially before I'd finished my basket.

I took another bite. "Better. Just had to get more into the burger."

"I knew you would think it was the best. Everyone does." He moved off down the bar and out to the other table of customers clearing away their now empty baskets after sharing a few words.

Kim owned a nice little business and he cared about what people thought. That came out loud and clear. His burger was pretty good. I wouldn't rate it as the best I'd ever had, but I wasn't going to tell him that.

Luke, the bartender from the night of the murder, strode in and went through the doors to the kitchen. He came out and went behind the bar and surveyed the customers. He washed a few glasses and then started cutting up lemons and limes wielding the knife like he was cutting the hearts out of vampires.

I finished the basket and the crispy fries, which were pretty stellar. He came down and grabbed the basket never looking at me. I wanted another draft to wash down my dinner.

Kim returned and noticed Luke. Kim re-entered the kitchen and Luke chopped harder making juice instead of wedges for drinks.

I wiped my hands on a napkin but realized they needed soap and water to get rid of the slippery feel. I rose and headed for the bathrooms near the door. As I was abreast of the kitchen door, Kim came out with a jacket slung over his shoulder and headed for the front door. As he opened it, light filled the small corridor and made me blind for an instant. Just as the door was about to close I looked and could have sworn Kim got into a black convertible driven by my uncle.

Chapter 23

KIM GETTING IN a car with my Uncle Rich unnerved me. So far Kim seemed decent except for hitting up his sister for money. He did say they were never close but did he lie when he told Luke he had something to do? If so, he did it well and I would be good to remember that.

As I washed my hands I wondered how best to get the bartender from Friday night talking about his boss and maybe something would slip.

I returned to my stool and tapped two fingers on the bar signaling for another beer.

Luke grabbed another frosty mug and filled it and traded it with my empty. He didn't seem interested in finishing his fruit juicing.

"You enjoy your job?" I knew I would get a response and I was glad he'd left the knife out of reach.

"Most days." His voice sullen. "Today's not one of them."

I nodded. "My boss sent me to Flatville against my wishes and it's been nothing but torture."

Luke laughed and actually seemed to relax. "I can't beat your week."

This was the opening I was looking for. The bartender seemed pretty chummy with Trudy. I wondered if he knew. Maybe I could subtly ask and get some information. He'd also been here the night of the murder and maybe he'd seen something that he didn't think meant anything but it did.

"So pretty surprising about what happened to Trudy?"

He shrugged his shoulders. I tried again. "You two were pretty tight, weren't you?"

Luke's eyes narrowed and the laughter died.

"I mean I saw you talking the night she was in here." I didn't want to say the night she was murdered. After all I was the guy who they thought did it.

He shrugged again. I let the silence hang for a minute and hoped he would fill it.

"She'd come in here a couple nights a week mostly when Kim was gone. I enjoyed talking with her."

I thought about her father who was sick.

"What did she talk about?"

"Nothing much. I got the impression she was coming in here to escape or take a break. She never stayed long. Just came in for a drink, never more than two and left."

"What do you think made her drink so much that night? She was pounding them back pretty good."

"I don't know. She always left if Ram ever came in. I know she didn't care for him."

"I wonder why?" I said it aloud hoping he would let me know what he thought. "They were always a pair. She was the Homecoming Queen. Ram was King."

I remembered my teenage dreams about Trudy in her red dress. You couldn't take your eyes off of her. She'd been a vision.

Luke just waited for me. He was a good bartender and knew that people didn't need anyone to respond to their problems, just a good listener. "What happened? How did they go from a couple to hating each other?"

"Oh, I don't know. I never asked and she never volunteered." Luke wiped the condensation on the bar from my first brew with a cloth.

"You talked to her the night she was killed? Why was she upset? What did she say?"

"I didn't talk to her except about her drinking. I told her to slow down. Kim told me that we had to watch our patrons. The cops were doing extra alcohol enforcement and if someone got pulled over for drunk driving and we'd served them, it would be reported to the Liquor Control Commission and he could lose his license. My boss truly cares about the safe driving of his customers. Not."

The last word was said with venom. Luke was not a fan of Kim, but then again he was called in on his day off.

"Let me see if I can find your bill."

As I watched him saunter toward the kitchen I noticed his perfect posture. I'd wondered if he was in the military at some point. The only others I'd see walk that way were cops who had to sit straight because of vests and their belt containing all their supplies like a gun, spare ammunition, hook for the flashlight and more.

Luke reappeared and punched a few numbers into the cash register. A couple moments later he slapped my bill down in front of me and moved off to another couple.

I threw some bills down to cover my meal and a generous tip. It never hurt to leave a big tip with a source you might have to come and talk with again.

Chapter 24

THE NEXT MORNING I didn't feel like hanging out at the paper. I spent some time in my room at the Shoemaker's making notes of what I knew and the conversations with Trudy's father and the bartender. None of it meant anything or led me to another suspect. I kept coming back to Ram.

Ram was a mean SOB but I couldn't see him killing anyone. But I didn't know him well now. Never did. My experience was limited to being a punching bag when I was younger and had no contact since to know Ram, the adult, except for what I'd seen at the reunion. It surprised me to hear Kim talk about Ram the role model.

Ram didn't have my brains from the gene pool. Maybe a stealthy-questioning reporter could trick him into letting something slip and confirm his guilt. I'd never known him to feel remorse when he beat on me as kids but I'd never known him to be physical with a woman. My uncle was even more of a mystery. His fronting the bail money surprised me. Time I renewed those family ties.

Maybe Ram struck Trudy after an argument. She wanted to break up or she tried to explain her need to spend more time with her father. Ram wanted all the attention. That could go with the boy I'd known. In a fit of rage and jealousy he killed Trudy. Maybe I could play on his guilt and get him to confess. I would need to get him on tape.

I searched my suitcase and found my voice recorder that looked like a pen. I didn't use it often but it came in handy for cagey sources, who clammed up when I pulled out a notebook. I loaded another notebook and my camera. I donned my blazer not wanting to have to stop by my lodging before my seminar this afternoon.

I walked the couple of blocks to the hardware store and studied it for a minute. The front had been recently renovated and a new sign with back-lit lights proclaimed "Malone Hardware." The front windows caught my attention with an attractive display of beach accessories arranged on a surface of real sand. Very inviting. The other window featured fishing gear ready to catch the big one next to the edge of a fake body of water.

I opened the glass door and a bell chimed. A dark-haired head appeared from a square island of counters accessible by a swinging door. Two cash registers were at each end.

"Can I help you?" The voice posed a question but the tone neutral. No obvious friendliness here.

I smiled. "Hi, Camelia. I didn't know you worked here."

"Hi Mitch. Good to see you." I could see her remember I was arrested for murder but she managed to keep half of her smile on her face. To cover her embarrassment she added quickly, "Since high school. It started as a great part-time job and I never seemed to quit."

"I thought you went away to school."

"Nope, couldn't afford it. I worked here for a couple years and saved and then got a degree in interior design mostly through night school."

"That explains the great window displays. You have talent."

She beamed. "Thanks. I try to create a new window on one side every week. You'd be surprised how many people come in and buy what's in the window."

"I wanted to buy a grill but then I don't have any place to put it."

She nodded. "Rich gives me carte blanche to do what I want."

She seemed pretty cozy with my uncle but she had been working for him for decades. "You the only one working?"

"Ram will be in this afternoon and Rich went to the bank. We aren't busy weekday mornings. We're all here on Saturday mornings. Those are a zoo."

I nodded. Great information if you enjoyed retail, which I didn't.

"So what does Ram do on his mornings off?" I tried to sound casual.

Camelia narrowed her eyes and looked me over.

"He and I never got along in high school. I'd like to see if I can change that." Sounded plausible to me and Camelia must have thought so too.

"Golf." She said the word like it explained everything. "He plays eighteen nearly every morning. Says it gives him fresh air and a clean conscious. Whatever that means. Should be finishing up about now at Flatville Country Club."

Wandering the nail and paint aisles seemed a waste of energy so figured I might as well continue to talk to Camelia. She'd been off my radar while in school. Seemed she always had a chip on her shoulder and I...I had other interests.

"You married? Kids?"

She shook her head. "I still have hopes." She glanced around the store to see if anyone was listening. "Ram and I are pretty tight so I'm hoping any day now."

"Well, congratulations. I wish you well."

"Thanks. It's going to be a big wedding and everyone in Flatville is going to be invited. My dress will be strapless with a big skirt and flowing train."

Camelia continued on describing her wedding but I didn't see a ring on her finger and figured she may have some delusions. If Ram was going to marry anyone it would have been Trudy but he hadn't done anything with that either since her divorce. Now Trudy was dead. Did that leave the door open for Camelia now to take her place? I wanted to ask more questions and distract her from the wedding plans.

"So have you and Ram been dating long?"

"We've been together for years, no one knows about it. We're together every day here and our relationship has grown."

I nodded. She seemed downright childish when talking about Ram. Scary. As I thought back I remembered she wasn't happy at the reunion and now I understood. Ram tried to drape Trudy all over himself. Interesting but I couldn't see Camelia killing Trudy. She was barely five feet and Trudy was at least eight inches taller. I needed to find out what exactly caused Trudy's death. So far via the active Flatville rumor mill touted shot, stabbed and beatened.

The door opened and Uncle Rich walked in.

"Mitch, my boy. How are you?" He strode over in two long steps extending his hand, grabbing mine firmly and vigorously shaking it up and down.

"Fine, sir."

"None of this sir business. Seems silly now that we're grown men. Uncle Rich doesn't seem quite right either, so why don't we stick with Rich?"

I shook my head yes and saw Rich cast a look at Camelia and tilt his head. She slunk away and started stocking some shelves.

Rich steered me toward the back of the store. On a table was a coffee pot, a box of powdered doughnuts and a popcorn machine that hadn't been put into action today.

"Coffee, doughnut?" Rich waved his arm toward the table.

"Thank you. I could use a cup of coffee." I helped myself to the hot brew that looked thick and added a doughnut, just for research purposes. These wouldn't be as good as the fresh ones I could get in Grand River but sometimes sacrifices had to be made.

"So are you enjoying your trip to Flatville?"

I snapped my head up from having sunk my teeth into the doughnut and felt powdered sugar litter my chin. Was my uncle nuts? I faced murder charges, not enjoying a pleasant summer visit or vacation. Was he struggling so hard to find a conversation topic that he'd grasped the first thing that came to his mind? He could have talked about the weather that was hot, humid and without a cloud in the sky but a storm was coming. The air charged with humidity and little wind.

"Not really. Everyone thinks I killed Trudy."

He seemed shocked by this. "I thought all that had been put to rest when you were released. They can't possibly think you did it?"

"My preliminary hearing is Friday. They'll lay out the evidence against me to see if a judge thinks there is enough to go to trial." I tried to swallow the blob of doughnut that had turned to cement in my mouth with his comments.

"Judge Roosevelt won't let that happen. He knows you didn't do it."

I wanted to be sarcastic and reply "Really. The judge won't let it happen. What about the cops and the other criminal justice professionals?

Do they turn their back because a local businessman has convinced his poker buddy of my innocence?"

But then I was used to the fair treatment in the big city of Grand River. Maybe in Flatville and Eureka County it was who you know. It offended me to have the charges dropped on Rich's principle. I believed in the justice system. Sure a few people got off, but I would rather go to trial than have the justice system skewed in my favor because I was the nephew of the hardware store owner. That was un-American.

I took a sip of the coffee. It was horrible and potent. I was sitting on a powder keg of a story. I get arrested and charged because of a law enforcement officer who hates me and piled up the evidence to look like I did it. I get the charges dropped because my uncle is a bigwig and friends with the judge. It balanced itself out but was wrong on so many levels. Here was my story that would beat the pants off Biff and Bob. Was everyone in Flatville a small step from crazy? Camelia wanted to marry Ram? My uncle thinking the charge would be forgotten? Not sure all that would fit but my uncle getting the charge dropped was news.

"I knew you would like that coffee. Being from the big city you're used to having coffee with legs. Can't find it like that anywhere around here."

Rich thought my smile was over the coffee. I would have liked to spit it out over the floor. I nodded to keep him from asking more questions about my glee. My mind spun with the work I needed to do, the people I would have to talk to in order to verify Rich's story, and get the information to make the situation come alive.

I felt the tingle and the rushing blood that comes from being on the trail of a great story. Time to say what I came to say and get to work.

"Uncle, err, Rich. I stopped to say thank you for putting up my bail money."

"Was the least I could do. Always intended on helping you out once you came back to town. I owed that to your dad but you never returned. I know you didn't hit that girl over the head and toss her in the river. You couldn't. You wouldn't. Now, let's not mention it again. Family is family."

My big story would be the charges against me being dropped because of who my uncle was. I would expose that and instead of being free, I'd have a great exclusive but back on the hook for murder. Many lesser reporters would have cringed but the story came first in my life. That's the way it was. If I was thrown in jail again, it was just another way to find a good story. I thought about the other guest in the jail. I also needed to find out what he was charged with. That would make a great side-bar story.

Rich slapped me on the back. "Don't you worry about nothing. Uncle Rich will take care of it."

I tried to breathe after the air whoosed out of my lungs with the force of the blow. Something wasn't right here but I couldn't figure that out now. I was on a hot story and couldn't wait to get started. Bells started going off but the blow made me lightheaded. I couldn't figure out if it was the words he said or the friendly tap on my back. Rich didn't know his own strength. He could hurt someone with very little effort. Could Ram have the same talent?

Chapter 25

I SAT IN the bar of Flatville Country Club in a dark, mahogany-paneled room that could put several studies to shame. Original paintings of landscapes dotted the walls between windows that showed great views of the first, tenth and twelfth tees and the eighteenth green.

I hadn't found Ram yet but was enjoying a full-bodied cup of coffee. The bartender in a white button-downed shirt with a green plaid bowtie asked if I wanted a refill.

We'd chatted about nothing much.

"Have you seen Ram this morning?"

"Not yet. He usually isn't in until half-past eleven." He motioned to a table by the window with a plate and drink already sitting there. His lunch will be served as soon as he comes in.

I nodded. "Does he order ahead?"

The bartender shook his head. "Always eats the same thing. Watercress sandwich, bowl of clam chowder and his Manhattan. Never changes and I've been here five years."

I sipped the warmed brew and felt the caffeine as if it was being fed intravenously.

"That's him now. The peach shirt."

I looked out at the eighteenth green. Ram putted the ball. A thrill went through me when it rolled right by the cup by a good three feet.

His face turned a mottled red that clashed with his shirt. Ram looked around but I didn't know his intent. Was it to see who noticed or if he was looking for a victim to unleash his anger? He started to raise his putter.

He was joined by Sam who I hadn't noticed by the golf cart. Sam said something and touched Ram's arm. The stiffness left his features. What had Sam said to create the transformation. It was an oddly-intimate gesture and I was almost embarrassed to have witnessed it.

"Doesn't Sam join him for lunch?" I said turning around to the bartender.

"Not usually. Ram eats by himself and stares out at the golf course."

"Any of that change this week?" I wondered if Ram's routine so pat that even the death of a close friend couldn't jar it.

"Nope."

"Did he ever bring in a date for dinner?" This was a risky question because it might bring up Trudy and the guy might recognize me.

"Sometimes, usually on Fridays. A blonde. A real looker. But I think they were having problems. The last few times they were in a couple of weeks ago they argued. They tried to keep it low but you could feel the tension. Bartenders know these things." He gave me a smile that said he was good at his job.

I nodded. "Only the good ones."

That seemed to please him. He folded napkins into triangle-shaped tents on the bar.

After about ten minutes my peach-shirted cousin appeared. Not many real men could carry off wearing such a shirt but I thought Ram did it well. He made the rounds of the room talking to several tables. He started to pull out his chair when he spotted me. I tipped my coffee cup to him. His hands clenched at his sides and the magic touch disappeared with Sam.

It felt good to make him miserable with just my presence. So many family gatherings came to mind where I would receive kidney shots compliments of Ram. He called me the whiney Malone and he was the strong Malone. I remember my grandmother patting him on the head and wishing it was me. I hadn't thought about my grandmother in a long time. She died long before Aaron.

So many things I had forgotten since leaving Flatville. Did I want to remember?

"Mitchy." The word wasn't a greeting. I'd come here looking for him and I'd found him. Time for him to see I was good at what I did. I didn't have some cushy job where I didn't go to work until afternoon. Time for a little poker and it was a good thing I brushed up on my bluffing.

"Dick, thank you for asking me to join you." The bartender finished filling my coffee cup for the third time. He'd done it to eavesdrop on our conversation.

"Would you add a club special for me? I'll be joining Mr. Malone." I clicked my pen to start the recording device.

"Right away, sir."

Ram frowned at his club's bartender probably because he called me sir. I was happy about that. My mission involved making him angry and losing control and see what spilled from the venom on the recording. I'd never understood why he'd hated me.

I picked up my cup and headed to Ram's table.

"This is a great view." I nodded to the eighteenth green out the window.

Another snarl from Ram as I pulled out the chair and sat down. He paused for a moment and then followed suit.

"What do you want?"

"Ram, you're my cousin. I want to reconnect, catch up." I tried for the most patronizing tone I could and an innocent expression. I'd even used his more preferred name.

"Cut the crap, Mitchy. What's your game?"

"Why do you hate me?" That wasn't how I intended to start but it slipped out.

"What?" Ram's Manhatten stopped its upward motion about an inch from his lips.

"You've always hated me. I wondered why." I sipped my coffee.

"I don't hate you." I could see the difficulty Ram had with the admission. He finished bringing the drink to his lips, taking a large swallow.

"Why have you always picked on me?"

"I was supposed to toughen you up." Another mouthful of the amber liquid disappeared.

"Toughen me up?" I couldn't believe what I was hearing. "Why?"

"Dad figured you would become a sissy with both your parents being eggheads. He called them too smart for their own good. He didn't want any sissies in the family."

My parents had been smart. Both had been full professors. My mom had even been a dean on her way to president or so my dad had boasted. He'd been happy teaching but mom wanted to influence policy. Funny how Ram's statements had triggered memories I hadn't thought of in years.

"Why?" Uncle Rich had never been negative, he'd even put up my bail.

He shrugged his shoulders. "You don't question my father. It can be painful."

The remaining liquor disappeared. He set the glass down and the ice hadn't even had time to soften the cube's corners. "I don't know. I was supposed to do it."

This didn't make sense. Part of me felt vindicated that Ram followed orders but another part pissed that they would even consider me a sissy. Maybe a bit bookish but that was because my parents made me read at least three books a week. I'd have rather been playing baseball with Scott and Aaron.

Aaron. I couldn't let that sidetrack me. I had to clear my name.

The bartender brought our food and paused a minute. "Will there be anything further?"

Ram lifted his glass and nodded to the bartender who looked surprised Ram varied from his habits. I hoped the alcohol would lossen his tongue.

"So why the hostility at the pub?"

"Old habits." He shoved another quarter of sandwich in his mouth and it wasn't pretty watching him chew but I could see he was thinking of a good answer.

"No. I don't buy it. There has to be something else." I'd spoken this aloud without realizing it. I leaned forward to ensure I didn't break eye contact with him.

"There you go again, using that brain of yours to figure things out. Why don't you go back to Grand River and leave us all alone? We were fine until you came home and stirred everyone up." He tore his eyes away and pushed back from the table searching the bar area.

The venom of his words betrayed his fear. Why? I needed to push just a bit more. My reporter instincts went on full alert. What was going on here?

The bartender appeared replacing the empty glass with a new one.

"I can't go home. I'm charged with murder, remember? Your buddy,

Sam, saw to that."

He paled and popped another quarter sandwich in his mouth and washed it down with good Kentucky bourbon and sweet vermouth.

I tried for a different tactic. "Why were you and Trudy arguing that night?"

"We weren't arguing." The denial quick, too quick.

"I'm trained as a reporter to pick up on body language even if I can't hear the words. You were arguing." I was channeling the Mitch who was doing an awesome job as seminar leader. Crap. I only had a few minutes left before I needed to be at the paper doing my seminar, but this was my reputation and my freedom. I had to find out if Ram was guilty.

Ram started for his last bit of sandwich but I grabbed his hand.

"Tell me now or do it on Friday in court. Your choice."

Ram blanched and set the sandwich back on his plate.

"Trudy was going through a tough time and wanted some help. I wasn't interested."

"That's not what I saw. I saw a bully manhandle her into submission." I let the words hang there.

"I'm not proud of it but I didn't kill her." Another gulp of amber disappeared.

"So why," I pressed hoping my pen picked up every word.

"She didn't want to live a charade anymore. Said she was tired of covering for everyone. She wasn't going to pretend to be my date anymore."

I let go of his arm and the sandwich disappeared. All color receded from Ram's face as he realized what he'd said. I got it too. The peach shirt, the intimate gesture, the fake dates.

"Her mother also made her promise that she'd take care of her father and never tell anyone he was sick. I didn't pay much attention when she started talking about her parents. I'm not proud of it but worried about my own skin."

I believed him. My heart sank as I relaxed into the chair. My only good suspect and I no longer believed he did it.

I started in on my sandwich and ate it nearly as fast as Ram. I was going to be late for my seminar.

Chapter 26

THE AFTERNOON SESSION at the *Gazette* had been a disaster. I was distracted and Bob and Biff took advantage. I didn't care. I had too many things on my mind. However, Scoop nearly slugged Biff when he made a particularly rude comment. Good thing she sat next to me so I could grab her shoulder before she did any damage. Biff didn't realize the danger he was in.

I managed to stave off a confrontation but only just barely. The publisher had skipped today's session so no one kept the duo in check. It was nearing four-thirty and I was ready to call it a day. We were talking about the finer points of interviewing techniques and the terrible twosome already thought they knew it all.

"To wrap up, an interviewer needs to be in tune with the subject's thoughts, feelings, goals, motivations and most importantly their body language. Only then can you tell when they are lying. Any of you play poker?"

"Poker, like that has anything to do with being a good reporter." Biff made no attempt to whisper.

Scoop's face started to turn red as she let her temper get the better of her. I motioned her back but couldn't make her relax.

"To be a good reporter you need to know when to bluff, when to fold and most importantly when a source is lying. You can hone those skills at a poker table."

"Yeah, when was the last time you played poker?" Bob thought he had me now. I winked at Scoop to let her know I had something special planned.

"Last Sunday. I took third place at the Texas hold'em tournament at the Flatville Moose Lodge. I could have gone for the top but was tired and had some reporting work to do."

"Must have been your lucky day." Biff tried to save face for Bob.

"Not so much. I'd only gotten out of jail for murder that morning I didn't even want to go and fleece the hardworking people of Flatville." I exaggerated just a little.

"Didn't mean I can't tell when someone is lying. You have to look for the 'tell.' I didn't get names, mind you, but the guy across from me squinted when he had good cards. The player to his left tapped his finger when any flipped card helped his hand. Should I go on?"

I stared directly at the two but they wouldn't meet my eyes. It was at a great place to quit for the day.

"Okay. See you tomorrow."

I watched as they all gathered their things and left the room. All but Scoop.

"Why didn't you let me tell those two numbskulls off?" Scoop demanded.

"That's not your job. Did you learn anything today?"

'Oh, yeah. I can read my dad pretty well but I need to apply those things to others. You should have let me get my dad. They wouldn't have been like that had he been in the room."

"Your dad has a business to run. I could handle it. Those losers will never get better than a second-rate paper."

Scoop looked stunned and I realized what I said. "Not this one but they will move on and it won't go anywhere." I needed to change the subject and fast.

"So what was your dad doing?"

"The police chief came in and demanded to see him."

"Really, does that happen often?" I wondered if he wanted a story held or giving some background information. Typically police chiefs went straight to the top if they were unhappy about a story.

"Nope. I hope Biff did something stupid. Maybe now dad will fire him. He's such a moron."

I walked to the door and Scoop followed. "Want to come for dinner tonight? It's chicken and mashed potatoes."

My mouth salivated with fried chicken and real potatoes. "Not tonight. I need to regroup and look at my murder defense."

"Can I help?" Scoop's eagerness was contagious.

"I'm not sure how. I have to rethink everything. The guy, who was number one on my list of suspects, proved to me today that he didn't do it. I need to regroup."

"I can help. You need someone to bounce ideas off." She had a point there but could I discuss my theories with a high school girl?

We were walking by the publisher's office and loud voices emanated.

"No, I will not." Scoop's dad's voice snarled.

The other voice responded in anger but was more muted so we were unable to make out the words.

"This is unacceptable." Again the publisher's voice, but wavering.

More discussion. Eavesdropping for background information is in a reporter's arsenal but Scoop was too emotional to go undetected. She would run to his defense and dress down anyone to defend her father.

"I don't like this," Monty said as the tiger became a kitten.

Scoop headed for the door, but I held her back. "Let it play out," I said in a low voice for her ears only.

Suddenly the door opened and as I turned Scoop from the door and said, "I can't make dinner tonight but thanks for the offer."

I looked up and into the eyes of Sam, mouth clenched, eyes hard. I wouldn't want to be a criminal with him working to put me in jail. Then I realized that was exactly what I was up against.

Sam pushed by us, and around the front counter then out the front door. Scoop rushed in to the office and I followed leaning against the doorframe.

The publisher looked old and haggard leaning forward on his desk, his cheek supported by his hand.

"Dad, is everything okay?" Scoop bypassed the desk and put her arms around his shoulders.

"Yes, honey. I'm fine. Just one of the down sides of being the top dog. That's all." He patted her hands.

"What did he want? Why were you arguing?" Scoop pressed like a good reporter.

"Nothing for you to be concerned with. I'll handle it." The color was coming back to his face as he took a deep breath.

"Oh, Mitch. Just the person I needed to see." I was in the doorway wondering if I should go or stay. "Sarah, you run on home and I'll be there for dinner."

Scoop hung her head at being dismissed. I understood her frustration at being treated like a child but couldn't do anything about it. I winked at her as she passed and received half a smile for my efforts.

I needed to talk to the publisher about nurturing Scoop's talents or face getting blindsided by them. I knew that day was coming, sooner rather than later. Her impetuousness could get her hurt and I didn't want to see that happen. She had the makings of being a great reporter, maybe not as good as me but close.

"Sit down, Mitch."

I sat and waited while the publisher collected his thoughts.

"We are going to cut your seminar short by a day or two."

I now knew what the argument was about. Sam couldn't afford to have me poking around. "Sir, I can't leave. I have a court date on Friday."

"My understanding is the charges will be dropped for lack of evidence. You will be free to go and I suggest you do it."

"With all due respect, I will find Trudy's killer. I don't want any potential charges haunting me for the rest of my life. It won't take long and the officers in Grand River will realize I'm still on the hook and ask for favors. I'm a reporter. I don't give favors." My barb had hit its mark, Monty straightened as he he'd been slapped.

"I understand Mitch, but, your services to the *Gazette* are hereby terminated."

"You can't." I interrupted.

"I can and did. I will contact the *Grand River Journal* and tell them to expect you back."

"What is Sam afraid of? What does he have on you?"

The publisher blanched at my questions but held firm.

"You can try and send me away but it is a free country and in most towns there still is freedom of the press. I will get the story here. Count on that. You might as well close the doors today. When the biggest story out of

Flatville lands on the front page of the *Journal*. People will figure out they don't need the local paper to get all the news. Mark my words."

"Mitch, you don't understand. My hands are tied."

"What does Sam have on you? Tell me. I can help."

The publisher shook his head. "It was a long time ago and best left forgotten."

"Not if he is controlling what goes in your paper. It can't be that bad."

The publisher's eyes hardened. Now he found his backbone.

"Son, it's time for you to go home." His voice was firm. He walked around the desk and pulled open the door that I now realized wasn't shut tight. I thought I saw Scoop disappear down the hall to the back.

At least I wouldn't have to tell her why. She would know. As I reached the door, I stopped and looked the publisher straight in the face.

"I'm disappointed, sir. I thought you were a newspaperman. I was wrong." With that parting shot I sauntered down the back hall and out of the building.

Chapter 27

PEOPLE WERE NERVOUS. That was a good sign, but I didn't know about what. I walked to Clive's office but he'd gone for the day. Time enough to tell him I'd been canned. Good thing my uncle had put up the bail and not the newspaper. I'd be in jail right now.

I walked back toward the paper and got my basic-black, nondescript rental car but I didn't want to spend any time with Harold and Kate and share I'd been fired. I was on edge and couldn't sit still for polite conversation. If I was in Grand River, I'd call Dennis, my friend on the police force and talk it over with him. See how a small town could make charges disappear. I wanted to call him but this wasn't his jurisdiction. I'd have to endure his teasing about the great Mitch Malone so stumped he had to call in the experts. At least he would get a good laugh out of it. Instead I found myself pulling into where it all began. The Main Street Pub.

The lot was empty. I decided to park in the middle because it was all sun anyway. I could see behind the building and down a gravel alley that ran the length of the block, parallel to Main Street. I sat there for a few moments running through the events of that night in my head. I'd come out and found Trudy behind the dumpster on the far side of the alley. Why had she been behind the dumpster? The parking lot was on the side of the building and an alley ran behind the building. The dumpster was down from the bar's back door which was a kitchen entrance. It was barely five o'clock and it was too early for the dinner crowd on a Wednesday. I was the only car in the lot. When growing up in Flatville, Wednesday was devoted to church whether it was choir practice, services, youth education and was the same for the Catholics, Methodists and the three Christian Reformed churches.

A classic green muscle car pulled into the alley and stopped by the dumpster revving its engine. To be young again, I felt middle aged today. Music blared from the speakers mounted in the back window, the bass vibrating. The car looked like the General Lee from the Dukes of Hazard reruns I watched at Aaron's. This car was green, not red and didn't have a Confederate flag on the roof. A little more sedate but still made for racing. I wanted a car like that in high school and my father had rejected it. My high school car had been a fifteen-year-old Volvo because it had the highest safety rating of its time. The most important fact when deciding on a car for my father.

I felt nostalgic and pulled out my camera and took a photo of it from behind. The car was in pristine condition without any rust or blemishes but was dusty from the hot, dry summer. What I wouldn't give to jump in it and take off leaving Flatville to eat my dust and just enjoy the open road. I'd never done such a cavalier thing in my life and I couldn't now with my court hearing looming in two days. Maybe I could find a muscle car on E-bay, but then I'd have to pay more for parking which was expensive in Grand River. I didn't pay to park my Jeep Cherokee now.

Deciding I also needed murder scene shots, I snapped one of the entry doors off the parking lot and one of the area with the wide-angle setting, shooting right from the car. I'd turned the engine off and opened the windows. I wasn't feeling that energetic to actually get out. The temperature neared ninety outside and even with the breeze the car would be an oven soon. I couldn't sit here long or I would bake.

I took a couple more photos of the car but couldn't see inside it because of the tinted windows. The guy honked his horn, like the loud music wasn't enough of a calling card. It was getting hot in the car and I tried to maneuver my navy blazer off. As I did I leaned over the passenger seat trying to free my arm.

As I came up, Luke, the bartender from the night of the murder, was halfway to the car and looking in the other direction like he was afraid of being seen. I had one arm in my jacket but forgot about removing the other arm as I watched. I'd once covered a story in Grand River about a pizza place that delivered marijuana along with the pizza. A drug delivery system operating under Sam's nose or maybe with Sam's help? Maybe that's why I made him nervous? Another good story idea. I had no idea what Biff and Bob spent their time doing. I found stories left and right or maybe they just found me. Were those two blind?

It looked like Luke carried a to-go bag of food. Good to know they did carryout. I grabbed my camera with my free arm and took a shot as the passenger-side window started down. I didn't think much would come of it. It was a long shot, but a good reporter is always aware and observing.

Luke leaned into the car and rested his arm on the door. I snapped another shot because it appealed to me artisitcially. With my angle, it didn't look like Luke had a head. I'd been fired from the job I didn't want and facing murder charges. Was I worried? No, I photographed comical shots of hot rod cars. How low could I go? I needed to focus on the murder charge. I needed to stop being a peeping Tom on a food delivery and figure out my problems. Besides, the temperature had risen in the car to egg frying levels. Time for a burger and a beer but maybe I should try a new place.

I reached down to start the car and get the air to cool my body and to encourage thinking instead of napping. I glanced back at the food delivery turning the key as far as the auxiliary setting.

As I watched, the pair exchanged words. Luke's angry voice drifted to my ears.

"You're not going to leave me holding the bag."

The bartender pulled back the paper bag and began to move away. "Call me when you have my cut."

I grabbed my camera off the passenger seat. Maybe I could get a shot of a fist-a-cuffs. Not sure even that would get my byline in the *Flatville Gazette* but it would give me another excuse to talk to Monty about letting me finish the seminars. I'd come here to do a job and I wanted to finish it.

I couldn't hear what the driver said but Luke leaned in again and started handing over the bag.

I wished the hot rod's windows weren't tinted. All I could see was a shadow waving something around. Maybe he was showing him an empty wallet and still wanted the food. I saw the movement but couldn't distinguish what it was.

I saw a flash and heard a backfire from an engine. The bartender stopped short. I took another photo as a reflex and watched the bartender sink to his knees, his shirt becoming soaked in a dark liquid. It wasn't a backfire I'd heard but a gunshot.

The green car's engine roared, spitting gravel and dust up behind it and I snapped the shutter again. The car took off and the bartender fell to the ground as I snapped another photo, the bag still clutched in his hand.

I jumped out of the car, my blazer flying like a flag behind me with it still in my left arm as I ran the bartender's side. I grabbed my cell phone putting the camera in its place in my pants' pocket.

"Help me," Luke's voice whispered.

I wasn't much on first aid but knew I needed to put pressure on the wound to stem the bleeding but squeamish about figuring out where the bullet hit. I'd been fired and didn't need the blazer anymore, rationalizing as I wadded it up. I pushed it on his chest. Blood pushed through my hands. Why was I the only one on the hot streets of Flatville?

I looked around for my cell and found it beside my leg. I used one hand on the wound and the other to dial nine-one-one.

"What is your emergency?" said a calm, professional voice.

"Main Street Pub bartender's been shot. In the alley. Behind the bar. Need an ambulance. Hurry. Bleeding profusely."

I set the phone back on the ground and used both hands to apply pressure.

"Hang in there, man. You're going to make it." My voice strained even to my own ears.

"No. I won't." The voice barely audible.

"Who did this to you?" A good reporter always asked questions.

"A lowlife drug dealer. Should have known better than to shake him down."

"Drug action in Flatville?" I daydreamed a story but didn't really think it was true.

"Make sure those drugs don't disappear."

"What drugs?" I looked around only seeing the paper bag of the take out food.

"In the bag." Luke's tone seemed a bit stronger but the blood poured from his wound in the upper left side of his chest.

"Who would take them?"

"Investigating the police department."

"Who's investigating the police department?"

"Me. I'm DEA." He was struggling for each word now but trying to hang on.

I fell back at the news but realized I needed to keep the pressure on the wound.

The cavalry was on its way or I hoped the sirens were coming in this direction.

"Open the bag and take a photo with your phone. Don't tell anyone. Trust no one." Luke's voice was getting soft. His breathing labored. "Trudy trusted you. Don't make my death mean nothing. Get the bastards."

Each word was an effort. He didn't know I had my camera. The sirens were getting closer. If I was going to do it I had to do it now. I pulled my camera out by the strap hanging out of the pocket. Letting go of my blood-soaked blazer and the pressure on his chest, I leaned back to get a shot of the bag and Luke. I knocked the bag over and it fell open showing small baggies of whitish powder and crystals. I didn't want to touch it. I'd learned my lesson on that one at a double homicide earlier in my career.

I took a couple quick snaps and then put the camera back in my jeans pocket making sure the strap wasn't visible. My hands returned to applying pressure to the wound.

As I did, I saw the flashing lights of a police cruiser enter the alley. The officer from my poker night stepped out in full uniform. He looked bigger and meaner in blue.

"What happened here?" He was business-like as he talked into the radio mike attached to his collar. "Where's the shooter?"

"Took off in a green car." I almost added that I had photos when the bartender's breath took a sudden intake, then gurgled. I remembered what he said. Luke's eyes burned into mine.

I didn't want to lie to an officer but didn't want to say more until I knew what was going on. I was already charged with murder. I didn't want this shooting added to my rap sheet.

"Can you help me, please? I don't know much about first aid." I knew most police officers had some training.

"Hang in there, man." My voice was urgent and I knew it would take a miracle for him to survive.

The ambulance arrived next and I was relieved of my charge. The faces of the EMTs grim, confirming my suspicion of how bad it was. More police cars flanked all angles.

I stood up and stretched. The blood dried on my hands in the heat, cracking with the movement. My white t-shirt was now dotted with red. I considered wiping them on it but decided against it. I didn't want to bother the emergency workers in their frantic actions. My cell phone was lying on the pavement. I didn't want that being part of the scene. I reached down and grabbed it marking my jeans with more blood as I shoved it in my pocket. At least it matched the other side where my camera was.

With the victim loaded into the ambulance, the officer returned from his patrol car and pulled me toward it. I needed to figure out what I was going to say.

"I need to get some information. Do you have any ID?"

"Yes, in my wallet." I went to reach for it. As I moved my fingers I realized how stiff they were. "Could I wash my hands? I don't want to get blood over any more of me than I have to."

The officer, whose tag read W. Walburga, grimaced. "Sure, but don't touch anything but the bathroom." He tilted his head to the kitchen door where the bartender had exited for the last time.

"Sure. I'll be right back."

As I got to the door I looked back. A dark spot coated the gravel where the bartender had laid. I started in and then took another glance. Something was wrong. The paper bag of drugs disappeared.

Chapter 28

EITHER THE OFFICER or one of the two EMTs must have taken the bag of money. I doubted it was the EMTS who had their hands full with their patient bleeding out. I needed to contact someone and fast or I could wind up with a bullet as well. I went into the restaurant but instead of going to the bathroom, I went to the bar and washed my hands in the small sink. I pulled my cell phone from my pocket and hit the first number on my speed dial.

Dennis Flarity and I had been friends for several years, as much as a police officer and a reporter can be. We respected each other and I had helped him solve some mysteries which enabled him to rise in the police ranks at the Grand River department. His phone went to voice mail. Just as well. I knew I didn't have much time.

"Dennis, Mitch here. I'm in trouble. An undercover DEA agent investigating the Flatville Police Department was shot and I'm a witness. The first police officer on the scene may have taken the drug money the agent was going to use to make the buy. I've got photos of the car but not sure who is the good guy here. Can you contact anyone you know who's legit in DEA? Oh, I'm already facing murder charges. Thanks." If I disappeared for good now, at least a real cop would know where to start.

I hung up and decided to wash my hands again and go further up my arms. I'd just put my hands in the sink when the officer appeared. "What's taking you so long? I heard voices. Were you talking to someone?"

"Just myself. Can't believe I found that guy bleeding on the ground."

"Let's get your statement." He turned and started heading back outside.

"Can't we do it in here? It's cool and I'm a bit queasy." The queasy was a lie but I was afraid I would be put in the back of the car and never be seen again.

"I need to control the scene. Please follow me."

I walked out and saw Biff, the police chief and the other officer who'd interrogated me. All three were stiff and rigid as they look at me.

I pulled my phone out of my pocket and wiped my bloody prints off it. I dialed my newest entry into the speed dial system. Clive answered on the first ring. "I need you behind the Main Street Pub. I'm about to be railroaded again. Hurry."

The phone was yanked out of my hands and the end button cut off my conversation.

"No phoning in an exclusive until we know what happened. I will not have you tainting an investigation. You hear?"

I nodded. Now was not the time to fight with Sam.

"You want to tell me what happened here?"

"I told it to your officer." I was trying to stall for Clive to get here. "Can I have my phone back?"

Sam thrust the phone into my chest as if it were his index finger and pushed hard to punctuate each word. "Do not release any details without my permission."

I nodded and took my phone.

"Walburga, secure the scene. I want yellow tape over the entire area. Why hasn't the state police crime lab been notified?"

Walburga turned red at being called out in public over his lack of following procedures.

Another car pulled up to the scene and Sheriff Whitaker Evans stepped out looking cool and collected. "Well, well, well, what do we have here?"

"This is in the city limits. Flatville will handle it." Sam moved to cut him of from advancing onto his scene.

"I'm just here to see if you need any assistance. I'm happy to provide deputies to secure the scene or handle onlookers." The sheriff's voice oozed helpfulness.

"I said we can handle it," Sam spit out.

"Fine, just being neighborly. Mr. Malone. We meet again. I just got a call. Seems we have some mutual friends."

My eyes must have looked incredulous and I couldn't think of a response.

"Dennis and I attended some FBI-sessions on firearms a few years back. He thinks an awful lot of you."

"Dennis is a good guy." I'd asked my friend for help and he sent me the sheriff—someone I could trust.

"You," Sam pointed at me. "Follow me."

We walked into the pub and sat at a booth. Before I had a chance to breathe he snarled: "What are you doing here?"

"I was coming in for dinner when the bartender was shot."

"By who?"

"Am I under arrest?"

"No."

"Then I would like to leave."

"We need your statement. We can hold you as a material witness. Don't make this difficult, Malone. I will not allow you to print any story before talking to the police. You hear that. Tell me what you know. Who shot him?"

"I don't know."

"I thought you were a witness."

"Mr. Malone. I would advise you not to say another word." Clive's voice terse. Each word struggled to get through his clenched jaw. "Chief, are you questioning my client without his attorney?"

The chief said nothing.

"You knew I'd been retained as counsel and yet you failed to contact me." Clive actually clucked his tongue.

The chief squirmed and I wanted to smile but didn't dare. This was serious.

"I would like a moment alone with my client." Clive motioned for me to follow him and we went out the front door and stood on the sidewalk.

"What happened?"

"I was coming for dinner and a green car pulled up and honked his horn.

The bartender came out and they were arguing. The guy in the car shot him but I couldn't see who it was." I sucked in a bunch of air and then continued. "I tried to stop the flow of blood but I don't think the guy is going to make it. He said he was DEA and to make sure the drugs or the money in the paper bag didn't disappear."

We walked down the sidewalk and past the entrance to the corner of the parking lot where we could see behind the building. Cops placed tented numbers next to items followed by a flash of light from the police photographer.

"Where's the bag now?"

"I don't know. I think Officer Walburga hid it. It was there one minute and when I looked after they loaded the bartender into the ambulance, it was gone." I shivered and it was ninety degrees out.

"No one is going to believe drugs were involved without evidence. This is a sleepy town. No problems." Clive rubbed the back of his neck as he thought.

"Won't the DEA guy have back up? Pissed federal cops that will come in and blanket the community? Take over the investigation?" I was running theories in my mind and voicing the most positive choices. There weren't many.

"If he had back up they would already be here. I'm not sure how they run their investigations but if he was in deep cover, they probably don't know yet." Clive shook his head. "Mitch, I'm afraid this is going to get ugly."

My cell phone vibrated in my pocket. I pulled it out. "I've got to get this. I called in some favors." I shrugged sheepishly while Clive frowned.

Clive walked over to the chief to discuss my freedom, I hoped. I pushed talk.

"Mitch?" The voice whispered.

"Yes, who is this?" I didn't need a deep throat informant.

"It's Scoop. I'm afraid something bad is going to happen." I could barely hear her.

Something bad already happened to me. "Why, what's the matter?"

"Dad got a call. Made him angry and scared. I don't know who it was but he is going to meet them at the newspaper in half an hour."

"Scoop, your dad is an adult. He knows what he's doing. Don't worry about it." She was getting paranoid. I looked around me at cops everywhere and a guy shot in broad daylight. Maybe paranoia was a good thing.

"You've taught me a lot. My instinct is he's in trouble. I'm going to help him."

I wanted to tell her that newspaper people don't get involved, only cover the news, but here I was involved in a shooting because I tried to save a guy's life. "What's your plan?"

"I'm on my way to the newspaper now. I'm going to hide in dad's bathroom, listen and find out what's going on."

This was so risky. I couldn't let Scoop do this alone. "Listen to me. Take your cell phone with you. I want to be on the line the entire time."

I glanced around and wondered what my chances of running interference for Scoop were? I looked at my phone and the battery was showing yellow. Not good on either account. "Call me back when you are in position." I disconnected to conserve whatever battery I had left. I needed to get out of here and get a different cell phone. I didn't have time to mess around with charging mine.

The lights and sirens had drawn a crowd of gawkers. I'd bet a shooting in Flatville would rate another special edition. Where were the reporters? I scanned the spectators and saw a flash. Bob tried to cross the police line but couldn't. At least he was trying to take some photos.

I walked over. "You want an exclusive on this?"

Bob look suspicious. "Why?"

"I need a favor. Give me your cell phone and I'll give you an exclusive."

"Exclusive of what?" He was clearly hesitant.

"I don't have much time." Scoop was working herself into place at the newspaper and would be calling me back at any moment.

"Bartender killed by gunman."

"Really? A major murder and I get the story?" Bob salivated but then stopped. "What's the catch?"

"The catch is you give me your cell phone now or the deal is off."

He reached in his pocket, pulled it out and handed it over.

"Now spill. I need details," Bob demanded.

"No attribution to me. You need to verify all the information through the cops. Got it?"

He nodded and I told him what had happened in a few quick sentences leaving out details about witnessing the murder, the getaway car, and the guy being DEA. I had to protect myself and keep information for my own exclusive.

For a small town, I found a hotbed of activity. Was all this going on when I was a boy? No, just boys being stupid and daring each other to jump when they shouldn't. I pushed thoughts of Aaron out of my head. That was old news.

Chapter 29

MY PHONE VIBRATED. I was back in my rental car, sitting, waiting for Clive to finish negotiating. The sun had dropped behind a line of clouds pushing toward Flatville bringing a stronger breeze. Rain. The police better work fast or all their evidence would be washed into the gutter. It was still hot but the air felt heavier and had lost its intensity without the sun.

Clive waved his arms as he punctuated his demands for my release from the scene. Sam and the other officials looked grim and unhappy but Clive wore them down. Sam pushed for a statement that I didn't have time for. I believed in justice but knew I needed to be there for Scoop. Something else was going on and it was coming to a head.

"Yeah."

"I'm in place. Dad just let someone in the front door and they are heading back to the office."

"Okay. Be quiet. Don't give your position away. Can you see who it is?"

I heard a quick intake of breath.

"What?"

"Mitch, I'm sorry."

"Sorry? Sorry for what?" I didn't understand why she apologized.

"It must be a false alarm. This can't be who is making my father so upset."

"Who is it? Remember your reporting. The least likely suspects are often guilty and get away with it. Stay impartial."

"It's your uncle. Rich Malone is meeting with my father."

Could my uncle be wrapped up in this? What was this? Drugs? Murder? I couldn't believe the man who paid my bail out of family loyalty could be doing anything wrong. He was a straight arrow just like my father. There had to be something else going on here. He must be upset about an incorrect advertisement or billing mistake. My uncle wanted to get it cleared up, although I didn't know why that couldn't wait until morning.

"Can you hear what they are saying?" I found myself whispering to match Scoop.

The silence stretched for a minute which seemed like an hour. Why was the publisher having a clandestine meeting with the owner of the hardware store? The thought still haunted me.

"Oh my God." Scoop's expletive seemed loud which had me worried. I didn't want to yell through the phone but she would give herself away and blow her cover. I wanted to reach through the wireless connection and wring her neck. She also wasn't giving me any details and I needed information.

Her voice was low, barely audible. "He's accusing my dad of black-mailing his son. Says he won't tolerate it. If any hint of a scandal hits the paper, he'll be sorry."

Wow. Blackmail? What had Ram done? I could believe Ram had done some shady dealings but I couldn't believe they would blackmail him because of it. Ram never understood the need for rules because he broke them when no one was looking. No one ever said anything which was as good as telling him it was okay.

I felt my breath exhale. This was simple. Ram had finally gotten caught and it was time to pay the piper. This didn't have anything to do with Trudy's murder or the drug deal. This was about Ram being stupid. That I could believe.

"My dad is trying to bluff. I can see it because he is pulling on his ear. He does it when he doesn't know what to say." Scoop would be a great poker player one day and an even better reporter. Lucky for me she was young and wouldn't be after my job for a few years.

"Okay, stay quiet and listen." I was beginning to relax. Scoop was all keyed up because this was her first operation. I was a pro, the teacher.

"Oh my God." Another expletive that wasn't a whisper.

"Scoop, you have to keep your voice low. They will find you and your dad won't be happy." I hunched over my phone, mimicking the actions she would be doing.

"Mitch." The word was said long and drawn out with horror. My pulse jumped forty points in a heartbeat. Something was wrong.

"What?" I screamed into the phone. I could hear scuffles and a large crack.

"He killed my dad." Her tone was level, even, belaying the seriousness of what she said.

"Who's there?" This from an angry voice I didn't recognize.

"Scoop, don't think about it now. Snap out of this. You must become a reporter. Come up with a story. Keep him talking. I'm on my way."

Scoop was in trouble. I started the engine and gunned it in the direction of the paper, four of the longest blocks I'd ever driven. If I had to, I was going to drive right through the front door.

"Oh, Mr. Malone. I didn't hear you. My dad makes me clean toilets to earn some spending money."

Good one, Scoop. Keep him talking. I'm almost there. I couldn't say the words aloud but I prayed them and hoped she got the message. The phone made a thunking noise and it was either my battery dying or she hid it behind the toilet.

"Dad is fussy about his toilets. Can't be any rust stains." Scoop was babbling but she was using her head.

I screeched to a halt in front of the newspaper, my car parked half in the road and half on the sidewalk. I hoped the cops got annoyed that I left and planned on following me. No sirens, no noise at all, not even birds or insects. Deadly quiet. Sweat ran down my back but I didn't feel the heat only fear.

I jumped out of the car and ran to the front door but it was locked. I saw Scoop heading out of the publisher's office. I couldn't see Rich or her father.

Then Rich appeared larger than life. Scoop saw me and started running in my direction.

I banged on the door and she skirted some desks. She had to clear the front counter and she could be out.

Rich was faster on his feet than I gave him credit for. He vaulted the front counter and stood between Scoop and the door. She tried to stop but her momentum carried her within reach of my uncle. He grabbed her pulling her in, then wrapping his arm around her neck to keep her from moving.

"Let her go," I yelled, pounding on the window to get his attention off Scoop.

Rich looked from me to Scoop and then saw my car. He pulled a gun and pointed it at my head through the locked glass door. Who was this man? He wasn't the uncle I remembered at family dinners.

I wondered for a minute what I was doing but I couldn't let Scoop be another casualty.

"I've got a car, Rich. I'll take you wherever you want to go." I tried to sound casual, diffuse the situation.

"Yes, you will." His voice was steel. None of the jovial banter we exchanged at his store this morning.

He pushed the crash bar on the door and advanced as I was back pedaling. His gun never wavered, nor did his grip on Scoop with his left. The gun was pointed at my chest, but I worried her neck could be broken with a lift of his beefy arm. I raised my hands like it was a stick-up, my phone still clutched in one. It beeped and I knew the battery was dead.

I saw Scoop's face riddled with fear and helplessness and I needed to keep Rich's attention focused on me but I needed to get Scoop free to call for help. "I'm not going to call nine-one-one or anything. Rich. Let's go have a talk. We can sit in the car."

"The police are busy so you are out of luck, Mitch. Chuck that phone or you and the girl are goners." My uncle's face was hard and set much like Ram's when he was about to punch my lights out.

I dropped my phone and it clattered to the ground, the battery flying out. Scoop used the distraction well. She stomped on Rich's instep, broke his grip and started toward me and I waved her off with my eyes.

"Get in and drive." The voice was low and menacing as he took a step and favored his foot. I wondered briefly if an alien had invaded my uncle and realized it was silly. This was where Ram got his mean streak and his propensity for violence. Why hadn't I seen it before?

Rich stood at the passenger door waiting for me to walk around to the driver's side, the gun never wavering and not allowing me to get close. Scoop had disappeared around the corner of the building and she was safe.

I got in. The car was still running. It must be only around eight but the sky was getting dark, the line of clouds now directly overhead. The thickening air was about to be unleashed. The clouds swirled and the one out front looked like an anvil, a thunderhead as mean and angry as Rich.

I wasn't sure if the storm was a good or a bad sign. I'd hated storms ever since Aaron. A thunderstorm had popped up while we were doing CPR and it got dark and cloudy, then the thunder and lightning hit. I'd sent Scott to call for help. Aaron and I were drenched and muddy by the time the rescue crew arrived. I couldn't be distracted by that teenage festering wound. I needed to keep Rich talking and me alive.

"So, where to?" I was trying for normal but my voice sounded flippant even to my ears.

"You were always the smart-aleck kid." Rich snarled. "I would have slapped you on several occasions but your parents wouldn't allow any sort of corporal punishment. Would have done you some good to take one across the mouth when it started flapping."

Ram's actions were now so easily understood. I'm sure his punishment for even minor infractions was painful. He pointed with his gun toward Main Street but in the opposite direction from the pub.

"Your parents mollycoddled you. Made you some egghead instead of a strong boy. My Ram was strong and tough. Where did I go wrong?"

Rich drifted with his thoughts and I scrambled to figure what was wrong with Ram.

"I've been cleaning up after Ram since high school."

What did that mean? I wanted to ask questions, but wondered if that would push him over the line into insanity and get me killed. I didn't want to die but there had been too many questions that had haunted me since returning to Flatville. The need to know outweighed the danger.

"What's wrong with Ram?"

Rich tensed, sat up straighter and brought the gun up to my head. Wrong question.

"Nothing is wrong with my son, just a phase. He's experimenting and will grow out of it."

"So Ram is doing drugs? That isn't something he will be able to kick on his own no matter how tough he is."

"Drugs?" Rich laughed. "Ram on drugs? Don't be ridiculous. My son wouldn't be so stupid. Now drive."

"So why are the feds in town investigating?"

"The feds are here?" Rich seemed surprised then his eyes narrowed. "Another complication. I'll have to fix it."

This wasn't going where I wanted. I needed to try a new track. I was driving down Main Street but Rich wouldn't let me go through downtown. I was headed in the opposite direction. I wondered where? Was he going to take me out to a deserted wood or stretch of road and then put a bullet or two in me? I needed to stop thinking about what was happening to me and my potential death.

"Uncle Rich…"

"Don't call me that." He was back on edge. My uncle was a psycho going from rages to calm in flashes. How had I never seen that before? I was still a kid when I left and we didn't socialize much with my uncle, mostly only on holidays. I hadn't been around him in a decade. Shouldn't I have had some indication in the last couple of days? I needed to be more observant.

"Why?" It was the best question I could come up with.

"I'm not your uncle." The statement was flat. No emotion.

"How is that possible?"

"Your grandparents adopted me. Your father never told you that? I was about eight and your father ten. I could never be as good as he was."

I was stunned. "My father or mother never said anything about you being adopted."

"No matter what I did he never treated me like anything other than a brother until I asked him for some money. Then I saw how he felt.

"I'd taken over the hardware store by then but it wasn't doing well. I'd tried some new things that hadn't worked. I'd invested in some land and the sale wasn't going to happen fast enough. I wasn't going to be able to make payroll. I only wanted a loan, but Timmy wouldn't do it." Rich laughed. "It was ironic. I needed the money for the land deal your dad was holding up."

I was trying to remember but the only thing that came to mind about family get-togethers were the food and staying away from Ram. Then I remembered the stories I'd read. It was Rich who was pushing for the school property.

"Said I had to learn from my experience. Your father gave me books to read. Can you imagine? Books. I came to borrow money for payroll and he gave me books on how to run an effective business."

I remembered that about my dad. Any time I had a question, he wouldn't answer it. Made me find the answer myself. He would help direct me and would even give me the book but I had to find the answer. I'd forgotten that. That was one of the reasons I became a reporter. To find answers.

"The only thing your family ever did for me was to force me to work in the hardware store when I was in high school. Every day until close I had to stock shelves, clean floors while your dad got to do chess club, quiz bowl and student council after school. I wasn't interested in that egg-head stuff so I had to work."

"When your granddad became ill, I made it so I took over the store. Your dad didn't have any interest. He only wanted to teach. Turn here."

I looked. It was the road that led to the back side of the bluff where Trudy had been found. I couldn't go there. That was where Trudy was murdered or at least her body dumped. Where Aaron died.

"Slow down," Rich barked.

I wanted to wrench the wheel into a tree but I also wanted to hear what Uncle Rich had to say. "They always loved Tim more than me. Tim got to go to the university. Tim got a cushy job at the university and only worked half the year. Tim had a classy wife. My wife, Jenny, got irrational after Ram was born. She didn't approve of my child rearing methods."

I remembered what my parents had told me. Aunt Jenny had complications during child birth that she'd never recovered from. I found out later that she had killed herself, but with this information maybe she had a little help.

He rambled and I tried to keep up and negotiate the road that was turning into more of a two-track with large pot holes. The impending rain would make it nearly impassable with the depressions filled with water. I heard the rumble of thunder in the distance.

"It's her fault that Ram turned out as he did. I tried everything to change him. I beat it out of him. I threatened. All it created was a rift and he's hid his sins."

I wasn't following anything. Was he so insane that he wasn't making sense?

"Sam will disappear soon. Then my work will be done."

I had to ask or I would never figure it out. "Sam? What did he do? He and Ram are good friends." I wanted to add partners in terror. I began to feel sympathy for Ram. He didn't have much of a chance with this crazy person for a father. The words my father had said when I had complained about Ram registered clearly. My dad had admonished me for being tough on Ram, talked about how difficult it had been and I needed to be understanding. We were family and there to help.

As if Rich knew I channeled my father's thoughts.

"Don't even start on your sainted parents. I was the one who bailed out the hardware store when our father couldn't manage it. Timmy couldn't be bothered. I took all the responsibility and he had all the fun." The words spewed like venom. "I took care of them."

I wanted to fight back, defend them but Rich held the gun.

As Rich talked, I realized that anyone in his way or who disagreed with him had disappeared. I thought of the "accident" my parents had. I'd never looked into it. Were they part of Rich's list of the dead?

"All of this is Sam's fault. If he wasn't such a needy boy, none of this would have happened. "

What? None of this was making any sense. The more Rich talked the slower I drove making big sweeps from one side of the road to the other, trying to delay our final destination.

"I will miss Sam. He was useful. So easily lead, so easily riled up. Never hurts to have the police chief in your pocket for all the inside information. I even recommended Wayne to him. Now there is a criminal."

Was Rich the reason Sam wanted to see me in jail?

"After the first kill, the others aren't bad."

Rich was changing subjects faster than I could keep up. I wanted to ask for a list of all the murders. I was running out of time until we got to the parking area and a sure death. I needed to make a plan to get out of this but I had to find out if Uncle Rich had a hand in my parent's death. I felt such anger and rage and was having difficulty not lashing out.

"How many people have you killed?" My voice tight forcing out each word. A plan started to come together in my mind. Maybe I could get out of this but I wanted answers too. A giant pot hole loomed ahead.

Rich seemed to think about that for a minute about his kills. I exaggerated a sweeping turn around the depression in the road, reached forward and turned off the passenger airbag.

"It started with Jenny. She wanted to coddle our son, make him a sissy. I wasn't fast enough removing her influence. She's the reason Ram is the way he is. I vowed never to make that mistake again."

Ram a sissy? I reached behind me and grabbed the seatbelt and started to move it forward, inch by inch.

"I always felt bad for the kid but he had seen them together."

"Kid?" My hand froze in mid pull. "What kid?"

"Aaron, I think? He came back to prove he wasn't chicken. He saw Sam and Ram. He called them gay. Taunted them that he would tell everyone at school that Sam and Ram were a couple unless they left him and his friends alone."

I hit the brakes. We weren't going that fast but enough to jostle both of us.

"You killed Aaron?" I screamed the words.

Rich brought the gun up higher, closer to my face like the jolt made him remember the possibility I could escape.

"Yes. Ram pushed him down in the dirt and then he and Sam ran into the woods. I couldn't have a hint of Ram's masculinity be challenged. I told him my son wasn't gay but he didn't believe me. I slapped him for his blasphemy. Knocked the wimp out cold, then tossed him into the river. It was so easy."

I turned reaching for him in a rage and got caught on the seatbelt I'd been trying to clandestinely hook.

"I always knew you would have balls. I could tell when you were growing up." The gun rose to my nose. I smelled carbon.

"You asked, Mitch. The good reporter you are." He was taunting me now. "I killed your parents too. I'm good at making things look like accidents." He laughed.

All the pain I had bottled up for years was welling up in my chest. I wanted to argue but the killing had been years ago. It should be behind me. Flatville had made it all return. I knew I didn't want to return. Why had I not stood my ground and refused this assignment?

So much misery by my uncle, scratch that. The man my grandparents adopted. He was no relative of mine. I wanted to use my fists on him and jab his face to bloody pulp.

I heard my father's voice for the second time in a week much the same way that Obi Wan Kenobi is in Luke Skywalker's head when he tells him to use the Force. I don't know if I'd blocked his voice by refusing to think about his death or refusing to grieve but I didn't have time to analyze it. It was the advice he'd given me every time I complained about Ram being a bully.

"Use your brain. Violence never solves a problem. You need to look at all sides of a problem, especially the other side and then come to it with logic and compromise. Only then will the problem be resolved and go away."

In light of the revelations about Ram I now understood his words and realized he had known, maybe he even helped Ram. Why couldn't I see that when he was alive? Now I needed to use his words to save myself and show this monster to the world. I fleetingly thought about my bet but that wasn't important now. Putting this bastard who killed my parents and best friend in the electric chair was now my sole goal.

A flash of lightning blinded us both and was followed by a crack of thunder.

"Get moving, reporter boy." Rich was all business. "I don't want to get stuck in any mud after I toss your body."

I knew what I had to do.

I casually put my seatbelt into place and took my time putting the car into motion. I'd stopped near a small clearing with a picnic table, fire pit and trash can. The woods became denser and then opened into the parking lot by the bluff. I'd have to make my move before the parking lot. But first I had one more question but I already knew the answer.

"And Trudy?"

Chapter 30

HE LOOKED PAINED. "That one was an accident. She was a lovely girl and would have made Ram a fine wife. She knew his secret and never told. I tried to get her to agree to marry him but she refused. I blackmailed her. Told her I would tell Sam her brother was dealing drugs. She said it didn't matter anymore. He needed help and maybe jail would scare him straight."

I wondered if I'd witnessed her brother's handiwork. The car I'd photographed earlier was her dad's hot rod that he didn't even remember he had.

"I tried to shake some sense into her but she fell. Hit her head on the counter in the hardware store. I'd called her and wanted to meet. Rich had come home after the reunion and told me Trudy refused to play his fake girlfriend." Rich was warming to his story, almost bragging.

The car barely made forward progress and I searched the darkened forest for a tree to suit my needs. Ram didn't notice.

"Told him she was tired of covering up for everyone and hiding secrets. People needed to get the help they needed. We agreed to meet at the store. Getting rid of the body was a mistake. Should have dumped her along a deserted road. The bluff had worked before. I didn't expect her to get discovered so soon. I was sorry to get you involved."

He wanted to kill me but apologized for my arrest? I had to make things right. Tell the world about my uncle, the killing fruitcake.

The trees were now closer to the edge of the road and it was like night.

Another round of lightning and thunder. The storm was nearly on us and would provide cover for me.

I gunned the engine.

"Hey, what—" Rich jolted from his memories of murder back to the present. We were bouncing and jolting with the potholes but picked up speed. Nearly to forty miles per hour. The perfect tree was up on the right. Forty-five miles per hour and I wrenched the wheel to the right. The right front quarter panel struck the tree. The noise of impact was deafening as was the jolt forward into the deployed airbag and then the recoil back. I gasped in pain where the seatbelt had held me from the windshield or where I connected with the power from the sprung bag.

I didn't think I was going fast enough to kill Rich. His eyes were closed and his forehead was ripped and bleeding. The windshield spider webbed where his head had connected.

I needed to get moving before he gained consciousness. I couldn't stay in this car with the monster I thought was my uncle. My need to run was paramount and adrenaline pumped my system with unreleased energy. As the door opened, big fat drops of rain pounded my head. I took one more look at Rich and hoped he would be unconscious until I could call in the cavalry.

The gun locked in his hand, his finger on the trigger. The gun started to rise. I couldn't wait. I had to go now or be another unnamed victim. For Aaron, for my parents, and for Trudy I needed to let the truth come out.

I turned my back on the car and ran down the road to the parking lot sliding on patches of mud but managing to keep myself upright and moving away from the madman with the gun. I didn't know if he was following or even capable of it. I heard a gunshot and with the rain and thunder didn't know how close or far away it was. Was he shooting at me? I kept putting one foot in front of the other as the rain soaked my clothes and impaired my vision.

Skidding to a stop, I realized I'd almost careened over the edge into the black river raging with the storm. This was where Trudy's body had been taken and where Rich smacked Aaron and thrown him in the river.

I'd avoided this area since his death. I'd carried boatloads of guilt for having left him up here and running off with Scott. Scott. I remembered the envelope he'd left for me. I needed to get with him and tell him it wasn't our fault. Had we stayed I knew we'd be dead now too.

I needed to tell someone to come and help me, then remembered Rich had chucked my phone. I frisked myself and found my camera in one pocket and a bulge in the other—Bob's cell phone. I was soaked and tried to protect the phone from the rain. It was worth it to let Bob have the murder story. I was too tired to write anything.

After dialing the three digits to summon help, I leaned against a pine tree that was devoid of branches for some fifteen to twenty feet but its upper branches provided some protection against the deluge.

"Nine-one-one. What is your emergency?"

"My name is Mitch Malone and my uncle, err, Rich Malone tried to kill me. We are at Green River overlook in the national forest by the park. My car collided with a tree. I'm not sure he is inside it or looking for me." As I said these words I moved to put the tree between me and the path so I wouldn't be immediately visible.

"Officers are en route."

"Please advise he has a gun and has taken one shot already."

"Do you know what kind of gun?"

"No."

"Where are you now?"

"On the top of the bluff's edge by the river."

I heard faint sirens but the noise muffled by the storm and the river crashing over rocks. The lightning and thunder were more distant but the rain was still coming down in sheets and it was dark.

Through nature's cacophony a branch cracked in the direction of the car.

"Sir?" I couldn't figure out where the voice was coming from until I realized I never had disconnected with the emergency operator. "Officers have secured the car and the passenger. An officer will be with you in minutes."

I closed the phone and put it in my pocket.

The noise was not coming from the path to the parking lot but from the path we use to use as kids that ran along the river.

I looked out and wanted to stay behind the tree. It was Sam.

"Mitch, I know you are here. We need to talk."

Did we? What could I say? I know your secret? Your lover's father was a mass murderer and you turned your back?

I stepped out and nearly lost a shoe that had sunk in the silty mud. I must have looked like a drowned rat. Sam was in some type of clear plastic covering his uniform and was wearing a hat with a shower cap over it to protect it from the rain.

"You okay?" He actually sounded concerned.

"I will be." I knew that was true. I'd learned some horrific truths that would change every memory I had about Flatville. How had one man committed murder of so many people I'd known? I could be bitter but oddly I felt relief. The crushing guilt wasn't gone yet but would be. I would never be able to go back and change it but maybe I could move forward.

"What happened?" Sam's voice brought me out of my self analysis.

I thought about all the bodies Uncle Rich had confessed to killing. How much needed to be dredged up? Aaron's parents needed to know the truth. I knew what happened to my parents. Trudy's murderer needed to be exposed and get my name off the suspect list.

How was all this going to affect Sam and should I care? I looked at him and realized I did. There had been enough anger and distrust in our lives. We were adults now and time to move on. Hate had taken too many people we'd known that should still be alive.

I took a step forward and realized my legs were shaky. A picnic table was in the middle of the clearing and I walked to it and sat down. Sam followed. I started at the beginning with Ram's mother and went through Rich's rampages against each of his victims.

Sam didn't interrupt. His face unreadable except for the pain I saw and anger but I didn't know at what. Was it me, Rich, the circumstances, how would this change his life?

Sam's first words after my tale were, "Rich is dead. The shot you heard was him blowing off his head."

He stopped and let that sink in for a minute. "I hope you got the insurance on the rental."

We both laughed. I nodded. "Company policy."

"Good to hear." We both had smiles, the tension broken.

"You okay?" I asked. After the words left my mouth I thought how stupid they sounded. I glanced around the clearing and realized the downpour changed to a drizzle.

"I will be. This is going to be tough for Ram. I knew his dad was mean and could be a SOB but I never figured him for all this. Sad. He was never happy. Always waiting for the next punch, confident he could never live up to his father's expectations."

"Did you know my grandparents adopted Rich? I don't think he ever got over that abandonment by his real parents. Always thought my father was a threat to the love they offered. In the end, he killed my parents because my father wouldn't loan him money for the store. He'd invested in some real estate deal." My voice shook.

"We need to get you back into town and into some dry clothes. This should be cut and dried but we need to go by the book. I'm going to need your clothes to send to the lab and make sure there isn't any brain matter imbedded in them."

I nodded and we headed toward the parking lot.

When we broke through the trees from the path, the multiple strobe lights of the emergency vehicles sparkled like a mirrored disco ball off the wet surfaces on the far end of the parking lot. As the bank of storm clouds moved further east, the intensity of the strobe diminished as the sky lightened and sun rays threaded through what was left of the clouds sending shafts of warm light before it would dip behind the trees. One hit Sam and me as we entered the lot. The warmth felt comforting. Good had triumphed over evil. I wasn't sure how much I believed in my Catholic upbringing but in this moment I felt a higher being warm my heart and a huge chunk of ice deeply imbedded melt. I paused and let the heat renew me.

I looked at Sam and back at the light through the clouds. Sam reached over and slung an arm around me.

"The worst is over." Sam looked at me.

I didn't flinch. He wasn't making a pass at me and even though I knew he liked guys, this gesture was a new start. We were adults now. Time to put those childish disagreements behind us.

"It is."

The comfortable silence hung for a few more steps. I felt a grin spread across my face. "I'm going to need to get some quotes from you on all this. This is going to make a great story for the wire service."

Sam stepped away from me and shook his head but the grin remained. "No comment."

"I made a bet with Biff and Bob that I couldn't find a major story in Flatville. I won."

Sam nodded then frowned. I'm sure he was picturing a headline something like this: "Local police chief outed in sex scandal with murderer's son."

"Don't worry. Cops don't tell reporters the whole story all the time. They only get what the police want the public to know. I have enough information to grab the headlines without all the details."

We walked for a few more steps.

"Besides you're going to bust a big drug ring in town and get all the headlines. No one is going to want to get rid of you."

Sam looked surprised.

"I'd go pick up Trudy's brother as soon as possible. I'm pretty sure it was him behind the wheel, although I never saw him. He shot the agent. Make him turn on whose supplying him. I think you'll find the drug kingpin is one of your officers. Wait a couple three days to let all this die down. Then you hold a press conference. I'll be gone by then and who knows, you may be a hero. No one will care after that."

Chapter 31

I HAD A story to write and went back to the newspaper to use their facilities. I'd forgotten all about Monty. Was he another one of Rich's casualties? I'd asked a cop who was just leaving. Monty had been knocked unconscious by a blow from the gun that had discharged with the impact. The bullet hit the ceiling. The wound had bled profusely but wasn't serious, a mild concussion. I was glad Scoop wouldn't be parentless. It had been a rough way to go.

My head swirled with all the death and destruction in one sleepy town. I didn't know where to begin. I always knew where to begin before. The lead and the first five or six paragraphs were constructed in my mind on my walk or drive before I ever sat down to wite. I was nervous. I couldn't shake it. Why was this bothering me?

Then I realized I'd never been the sole reason for death and destruction before and it had never been at the hands of someone I'd known or cared about. Granted Uncle Rich and I weren't the best of buddies but he was my uncle. I'd known him all my life. He'd sat across the table at every holiday while I grew up.

So had Ram and I never knew. My dad had known. I felt ashamed for all the times I'd thought ill of Ram and never looked for a cause. Granted he terrorized me but he had his own nightmares to deal with that were much greater compared to what he had done to me and my friends. His father had been a psycho and killed his mother. I wondered if Ram knew? If not, he wouldn't be hearing it from me.

A lead paragraph was starting to come together in my mind. I still wasn't comfortable writing about my family's sins but I was a newspaper reporter. A job was a job. You couldn't pick the subjects or stories you covered.

An officer had dropped me off at the newspaper as I requested. Every light in the place shone onto the glistening, wet sidewalk and the front door wasn't locked. The place had never had so much attention or activity on a Wednesday night before.

I opened the door and expected only Biff or Bob to be working. The newsroom bustled with people working on what appeared to be stories. Maybe my seminars had paid off and they were more dedicated to the job as they understood what the possibilities were. I moved into the room and toward a computer used by the lifestyle editor, the only one open in the newsroom where reporters were typing furiously as they neared their deadline but in reality had more than twelve hours to go.

I was nearly to the desk when I heard the scratches of fingers hitting electronic keyboards pause. It didn't register for a moment but then the sound of applause did. I looked around. I had been intent on getting to a computer and focused on what I would write when my fingers encountered the keyboard.

I stopped and looked. They all had stood up and clapped. Bob came over and raised my hand up in the air. "Ace reporter Mitch Malone. Not only does he find the biggest story of the century in a sleepy town but puts his life on the line to see justice done."

"I…" I didn't know what to say. "I have a story to write." I stammered as I pulled my arm back and went to the computer. I felt like I was in a fishbowl but I didn't want their attention now. I was totally focused on my story.

The words poured out of me. I must have been typing furiously for over an hour. I stopped, drained. It was nearly one o'clock in the morning and I went in search of a cup of crappy coffee. It was going to be an all-nighter and a year's worth of adrenaline had been burned tonight. My well empty.

I walked to the break room and got my brew. The thick, dark brew tasted nasty, but would do the job. I needed to move my stiffening limbs until I was ready to go back to the keyboard and let the caffeine take over my system.

I wandered to the back by the press, surprised the entire area was lit up in fluorescent lights. I heard banging and what sounded like metal on metal. It wasn't a good noise. I went around the press to the backside.

Scoop had a wrench in her hand and continuously hit the metal support. Tears streamed down her cheeks. She paused then muttered, hiccupped and wiped her face with her sleeve that was transferring either ink or grease to it making it look like the black lines under football player's eyes on game day. She raised the wrench to continue her assault.

"Scoop?" My voice was soft. I didn't know if I wanted to interrupt her rampage. Would she take the wrench to me?

"Mitch?" Her eyes were incredulous. She dropped the wrench and ran to me. Her face planted in my chest, her arms snacked around my midsection. I still held the coffee cup and tried to keep the steaming contents from spilling and burning her but I managed to put one arm around her. It was enough.

She babbled and cried harder. I couldn't make sense out of it. I let her go on. After a few minutes her frenzy slowed and I pushed her away.

"Let's talk."

I steered her out the door to the back employee parking lot. I motioned to a cement barrier that marked a parking place. It was dark and peaceful and the air smelled clean from the storm earlier.

She sat and so did I. What passed for coffee was now closer to lukewarm than hot. I took several long gulps trying to figure out what to say.

"Good reporters don't get emotional." It was the only thing I could think to say.

"That's just it. I can't be a reporter." Her voice husky and deflated.

"Why?" What had happened to change her career choice?

Scoop sucked in a huge breath bringing with it a massive amount of drainage that echoed in the dark lot. She swallowed it down. Then hiccupped.

"After all the cops had our statements and did their crime scene, dad sent me back to work on the press and make sure it was up to printing a special edition. He wants it to hit the streets at six just as people are getting ready for the day."

Sound newspaper judgment. A special edition explained why the newspaper was lit up like a Christmas tree and all hands on deck. Scoop wasn't done yet.

"Yes. I was part of the story and I can't even write it. I'm supposed to be interviewed by Bob."

I saw the problem. Scoop was a true newspaper reporter through and through. I couldn't recognize a psycho in my uncle, but I could fix this.

"Skip Bob. You need to get yourself presentable. Reporters never look like football players."

She looked at me with a question in her eyes.

"You have a story to write and if you don't want to, fine. Where's your dad?"

"He went home to get a couple of hours of sleep. His head was killing him."

"Then we don't have much time." I stood and held my hand out to Scoop and pulled her to her feet. "You hit the restroom and try to get that ink off your face and get rid of that apron. Then meet me in the newsroom."

She looked like she was about to protest but I wouldn't let her. "Go. Trust me."

She did as I asked. Now for my work.

I returned to the newsroom.

"Okay, listen up." I had everyone's attention. Even Biff and Bob. "We need to do a little coordination of coverage so all our stories aren't the same. Bob, what angle do you have?"

"I'm working on the murder at the pub."

"Great. Biff?"

"I'm writing the police angle," he paused wondering what to say about the tragedy of my family.

"It's okay, my uncle was a lunatic, no sugarcoating that. You might want to head back to the police department and see if they have more information. Their officers should be finishing their reports and you want to get them talking before they go off shift." Biff looked like he wanted to argue but grabbed his notebook and took off.

Perfect. Now I had a computer for Scoop to use. I saw her in the door. I motioned her in and had her take the computer I'd been using. I would shift to Biff's.

"What do I write?" she whispered.

"You are a reporter. What did you witness?"

"Someone else is writing all that, mine won't get in the paper." She was sounding like a two-year-old.

"Just canvassed the troops and no one is covering what went on here. Maybe you could take the angle of what happens when violence knocks at the newspaper."

I saw a gleam in her eyes and without a word she turned her back on me and began typing.

I went over to Biff's computer and started work on a sidebar about Trudy. It was long past time for that woman to be recognized for all her work.

I just hit the last paragraph when Scoop's dad walked in.

"How's it going? I'm expecting great writing on this." His voice was hale and hearty and the only indication of his injury was a white piece of gauze from his right eye into his now shaven hairline.

"No concussion?"

"Just a headache. I'm fit as a fiddle and ready to start reading some copy. I'm pleased to have you aboard, Mitch."

I saw Scoop slink lower in her seat. I had no idea what Scoop had written or if she had talent. She did have the nerve and maybe that was more important than the writing. She was also a rookie.

I got out of my seat. "Monty, can I talk to you a minute." I steered him towards where Scoop was working but I positioned him with his back to Scoop. I hoped Scoop understood what I was doing. I tried to catch her eye over Monty's shoulder but she still hunkered down.

"Sir, I'm curious. Why did Rich Malone come here?"

"He wanted to talk about advertising. I didn't think anything of it." I knew Monty was lying. There was something between the two, some hold Rich had but it had died with him. Monty was smart enough to know that.

"At what point did your newspaper sense start to take over?" I flattered him hoping he would open up a bit. I wasn't taking notes so he may have felt more comfortable talking.

The flattery worked. He started talking and as he got into his story the better it became. I also was able to move and see Scoop typing away as he talked. She would have some great quotes to go in her story now.

Monty wound himself out and then headed for his office to begin reading. Biff was coming back and I cleared out of his work space. I saw Scoop's hands appear over the top of the cubicle and saw her stretch and probably yawn. The adrenaline from the day was gone. Time for the teacher to go to work.

I stepped into the cubicle and felt her tense. She knew Biff was back. "It's okay. Let's see what you have."

She moved over in the narrow space to allow both of us access to the screen. I scrolled up and started reading. Scoop had potential.

I started making some changes here and there but she captured a normal meeting gone wrong. She laced the publisher's comments in as well as her own observations. I explained what I was doing and why.

"Great job! You forgot one thing." I scrolled to the top and started typing, then paused. "Have you decided how your byline is going to read? Scoop, Sarah?"

I looked back at her and she was beaming. "S.E. Bradshaw has a certain ring to it," she said with a saucy grin.

"That it does." I typed it at the top. "Ready?" I had my finger poised over the key that would send it to the editing queue where her father would read it. She nodded and it was gone.

"How about some breakfast? You got any decent place to get doughnuts around here?"

Scoop smiled, grabbed my arm and pulled me out the front door of the paper.

Chapter 32

AFTER A HALF dozen doughnuts from the local grocery store, I was feeling a bit better and needed to finish up at the paper and then get some shut eye.

The minute we walked in the door I knew we were in trouble. The publisher was at the door to his office.

"Malone! In my office now and bring that protégé of yours as well."

This wasn't going to be good. I could tell by the voice.

We followed him into his office and he shut the door behind us.

"Scoop, is the press ready?" He was seated behind his desk but we were standing in front of it like recruits in front of the drill sergeant.

"Yes sir." Her eyes were on the carpet and her voice more of a mumble.

"Malone. Who runs this newspaper?"

"You do, sir."

"Yes, I do. I decide who writes stories and who comes to work here."

"Understood, sir." I wanted to add a salute but decided I needed to toe the line for Scoop's sake.

"Now that being said, Sarah." His voice softened.

I looked at Scoop, who was staring at her shoes.

Her father moved to her and lifted her chin. "Your story brought tears to my eyes. You have talent. It reminded me of your mother."

There were real tears in his eyes. He wrapped his arms around her. "Didn't need any changes. I bet you had some help with the editing."

She nodded and glanced in my direction.

"Scoop, I wanted so much more for you than a newspaper life. I learned tonight that you can't control life or how long you have on this earth." He gingerly touched his bandage. "I won't oppose your choice of schools or careers, but with one caveat. Until you return to school, I will expect regular stories from you. You can start by filling in for Biff on the police beat. He's going to be taking a week's vacation."

Scoop flew into her father's arms. "I love you, Daddy."

A tear came to my eye and I had to look down. Other eyes glistened as well.

Monty cleared his throat and set Scoop in front of him. "You will need to go on rounds with him today and allow him to show you the ropes. Got it?" He'd tried for being a gruff, professional publisher but realized he'd failed. Monty wrapped his arms around his daughter and kissed the top of her head.

"Yes, sir." Enthusiasm filled her reply.

My work here was done.

"Now, the first plates should be ready, would you please help with the press until your new assignment starts this afternoon?"

"Yes, sir." She left the room her feet barely hitting the floor.

I turned to follow.

"Mitch, a moment please."

I stopped and turned around to face him. He motioned to a seat and I sat.

He went around to his desk and sat, the leather chair creaking as his bulk settled in.

"Thank you. I didn't think Sarah was interested in being a reporter except that she wanted to remember her mother. I see now that she has the same itch her mother had. I owe you for that."

I nodded.

"I also wanted to thank you for the marvelous job you did with the seminars. I didn't get to be in all of them but I can see the result. I didn't have to call a single staff member in for this extra we are doing. They all knew what to do and from the copy I read, they took to heart your suggestions. I've no doubt we will win some awards for this coverage."

Again, I nodded. I'd appreciated the gesture but had the feeling there was more. Monty steepled his hands so the fingers met at the tops.

I was beginning to feel the exhaustion and wanted whatever he said to be over so I could get some shut eye. Another doughnut might help but I wanted sleep. I was spent.

"Mitch, you weren't in Flatville by accident."

I swung my head up. What did he mean by that?

"Trudy came to see me a couple of times and tried to see if you would come back for a visit. She wanted to talk to you."

"Why didn't she write?"

"My impression was she had but you never answered."

I didn't receive any personal letters. I never did. I had no idea what he was talking about.

"She talked about what a great reporter you were. Had apparently followed your career in Grand River."

Wow, that was amazing. I didn't even think she knew who I was.

"She wanted your help with something and wanted me to get you here. I admit I hesitated at first but after the third visit I could see she was right about the newspaper being tired and needing an infusion of enthusiasm."

"I never figured Trudy for an expert on newspapers." I reeled from his revelation.

"I don't think she was but she was smart. I think she allowed everyone to think about her as spacey but not much got by Trudy. She wanted you here for something and whether it was help with Ram, or his father or something else, I don't think we will ever know."

That was true enough. She had a mess on her hands. The publisher didn't even know yet about her brother. That reminded me I needed to send some photos to Sam and then maybe I would shoot an email to Scoop after Kim was arrested.

I was feeling generous. I'd won the bet and then some. The Homecoming queen did want me and I was going back to Grand River where I belonged. Flatville was a nice place to visit but I wouldn't want to live here again. I'd have to return to testify if things ever got that far, but my week teaching was done. I was so good, I didn't need all five days.

I'd survived. Maybe in five years I would come to the next reunion.

I was Mitch Malone, former Flatville resident, and I was back on my Grand River crime beat. Scoop would keep the locals on their toes.

Epilogue

THE MAIN STREET Pub had closed Friday night to the public. Trudy's brother, Kim, offered to hold a memorial service for his sister.

I'd arrived early to make sure everything was set. I felt responsible in a small way. Trudy had wanted me here to help her and my uncle cut it short. The least I could do was see that the celebration of her life fit with the woman who kept so many secrets at such a great cost. Her father was deep in the throes of Alzheimer's disease. The Shoemakers had contacted his physician. Trudy had done everything she could medically for her father and nursed him as best she could. Now she was gone, the doctor recommended a nursing facility. They were working through the process to get him a room but there was a waiting list.

I was glad that Trudy's biggest worry would be taken care of. She didn't want to return to Flatville but circumstances forced her. I felt her pain.

Again, the Shoemakers had done a great job. Three square tables pulled together and connected by a single tablecloth had been set along the wall by the entrance. They'd taken photos from the walls of her father's house and set them around the area. They'd placed a guest book and a jar for cards and memorials.

They'd talked to her father in a moment of lucidness and told him about Trudy. He'd cried and grieved. He suggested a scholarship in her name to Flatville High School. Any donations collected would be used for that purpose. Her body had already been cremated and placed in the plot with his wife. There was still room for him as well. Then he'd slipped into his mind, away from the pain and repeating happier days over and over again.

I slipped into a back booth, but not fast enough.

I'd wanted to connect with Scott. I'd only recently looked at the envelope he'd left for me at the *Gazette*.

It was a copy of Aaron's autopsy report. I'd read the grim medical speak before for stories so I knew what I was looking at, but not ones where I'd done CPR.

I scanned the document looking for the pertinent details. "Bruising inconsistent with hitting rocky projections." I looked further. "Post-mortem bruising revealed the shape of a hand on victim's left cheek."

I scrolled down farther through the medical jargon. "Fluid present in lungs consistent with drowning." Then in the notes was "bruising on the cheek consistent with an ante mortem blow similar to a large hand. Victim likely was unconscious when he entered the water."

I knew whose hand had made the bruising to Aaron's cheek. I wish I'd taken the time to talk to Scott when he dropped it off.

Scott and I had shared secrets so many years ago but I didn't know the man or how the past had changed him. I wasn't going to be staying in Flatville and wondering about renewing the friendship, but first I needed to explain what happened.

"Scott. Good to see you." I stuck out my hand and we shook. I pointed to the other seat and he took it. "I read the report you gave me." I started not sure how to approach the subject.

"I work at the Medical Examiner's office and looked through the files once and found it. I wondered what had happened after we ran off." He stopped then added with a softer voice. "Wished I'd stayed with him that day."

"Me too." The silence fell and we each stared at the table looking for answers and finding nothing but the wood grain. I didn't want to discuss this but I knew what happened and Scott deserved to know.

"Ram's father killed Aaron." Blunt but I had to get it out there.

Scott's head came up fast, his mouth falling open.

"In the car on the way to the bluff, when he planned on killing me, he gloated over all the deaths he had gotten away with. Aaron was his second. His wife was the first."

Scott's eyes became round, stunned. He'd had time to come to terms with Aaron dying. We had each been with Trudy right before her death and that connection was still raw even though neither of us was close to her. I thought fleetingly of Sam but would deal with him later.

"I'm not sure how much of this will come out for the general public but I want you to hear the whole story. Aaron taunted Ram and Sam after we ran down the path. Rich was coming up the path and heard it. Ram went to get in the car and Sam raced past us, but Rich stayed back. Apparently Aaron wouldn't promise to keep quiet so Rich hit him. It stunned him or knocked him unconscious and Rich threw him over the bluff. Knowing how strong Rich was, Aaron could already have been dying, but the water finished him off."

I took a deep breath after my little speech. I wanted it all out there. I decided to not say anything about Ram and Sam's secret. When they were ready to come out of the closet, they deserved to do it on their terms.

We changed the subject and didn't talk of Aaron's death anymore. What we did talk about was all our adventures with Aaron. The fun we'd had, happy memories.

Trudy had been kind to many people, and ultimately it had caused her death, but because of her, Scott and I could move on.

"I've got to get going. Was sure great talking to you, Mitch. Let's keep in touch." We shook hands. He shuffled toward the door and stopped to drop something in the memorial jar.

I was glad that was over.

I thought Trudy would approve as I ambled to the bar and ordered a draft. My mouth was dry and more people were coming in. There wasn't a program for the memorial but more of an open house. I saw the Shoemakers arrive. I planned on pulling out of town first thing in the morning and thought I would say my thanks now.

I grabbed the frosted mug and headed in their direction. Kim was providing the alcohol. Said it was the least he could do for his sister.

I tensed. Ram entered looking subdued in gray slacks and a white golf shirt. His hair slicked back. I hadn't heard anything about a service for his father but I didn't think I would be attending.

The coverage in the *Gazette* had convicted him in the murder of Trudy but was a bit sketchy on the details. Those police reports just don't give the information to make a full disclosure in the press. None of his other deaths were reported. I'd already gone to Aaron's parents and told them what had happened. I'd explained about their son sticking up for his friends and refusing to give in to a bully. He had just been in the wrong place and the wrong time. I thought it helped but they would always grieve for the son they'd lost but now at least they knew the exact circumstances. Maybe they shared in some guilt over letting him have so much freedom.

I'd not talked to Ram since his father's death. I wasn't sure what would happen.

The silence lengthened, each of us trying to figure out a way to start a normal conversation and being unable too. "Sorry about your dad" was the best I came up with.

"That's okay. I'm sorry he put you through that and all the damage he's done."

Now that Ram was talking it was like a dam had burst. "I thought I'd seen changes in him and was encouraging him to see a doctor but he wouldn't listen. The autopsy showed signs of a tumor in his brain. They can't be sure because of the gun blast but thought maybe his latest more irrational behavior had stemmed from pressure by the tumor. We'll never know.

"Mitch, there is a matter I need to discuss with you." He shifted uncomfortably. "I want to thank you for not divulging my secret. You could have easily without any thought as part of your story. I've been going through dad's papers and have encountered a few oddities."

I wondered what they were. I'd not told anyone about Rich causing my parents accident. There was enough grief and guilt and it didn't matter. I knew. I was not comfortable with this new softer side of Ram and wanted to get away.

"It seemed when dad probated your parents' will, he took a loan from the estate to remodel and improve the hardware store and help with cashflow. There was some land deal that involved several people in the community that didn't proceed as planned and he was over extended." He paused to catch his breath.

Land deal huh? Ever the reporter I wondered if it was property for a new school. I also wondered if the other investors were Monty and Judge

Roosevelt. That would explain a few things.

"According to the paperwork, you have an interest in the store. Do you want to run it?"

I owned a piece of the store? I couldn't wrap my head around that. I'd never been business oriented and wouldn't know the first thing about it. I looked around the room that was now filled with people talking and laughing and shedding a tear or two as they talked about Trudy.

I had a great life in Grand River. I didn't need the money or income or even the hassle. I was a crime beat reporter and I didn't want a desk job and I didn't want to own part of business.

"Thanks, Ram. That's a really generous offer but I'll have to pass. Why don't you put my share in the scholarship fund for Trudy? My parents would approve of their estate helping to fund college educations for deserving youth. They were very big on improving the mind.

"Are you going to stay with the store?" I wanted to get away from the death of his father.

"For the short term. I was never interested in it. I'm going to put it up for sale, I think."

I nodded. Ram had suffered several shocks over the last few days and needed time to think and figure out who he was and not who is father tried to create him to be.

"Why don't you put the store in some quality hands for the short term while you figure it out?"

"I don't know anyone who knows the business."

"What about Camelia? When I talked to her I got the impression she'd knew its workings from top to bottom. Put her in charge and see what happens. If it begins to fail, then adjust. Maybe she can buy it from you after a probationary period."

"Camelia, huh? I've spent so much time ignoring her I never gave her a thought." I could see him considering it. Camelia wouldn't get the man of her dreams but she would get the store which was what she'd been working hard at for years. A thought struck me. Maybe I could get her another man of her dreams or at least someone to help her with the store.

Ram stood, sticking out his hand. I followed him to his feet. We shook and were finally grown up.

I wandered around a couple groups of people, surprised to see the sheriff. He motioned with his head and we separated from the group and went toward the bar.

"Good to see you without the cuffs." The words were light but I sensed there was more he wanted to say.

"Yes, the weight was overwhelming. I've been meaning to ask you why you were included in my questioning."

"I was claiming her death occurred in the county, not in the city. I looked to grab some headlines and keep my finger in the investigation. I'm coming up for re-election in a year or so. Getting a free photo in the paper is just good politics."

"Great answer." I grabbed some peanuts off a dish on the bar and chewed them. "Now how about cutting the bull and telling me the real reason."

"Mitch, I'm offended. The body was found outside the city. The bluff is in the county's enforcement area."

I just held his gaze. "This isn't for print. My stories for the *Gazette* are done. I'm heading out of town in less than twelve hours."

"I knew someone was tipping off the drug dealers about busts. We worked with the DEA and knew about it." The Sherriff glanced around and lowered his voice making sure he knew where Kim was. "This is off the record. I will deny it if it ever appears in print. I knew it was an officer and had checked mine and they were clean. I wondered if it was Sam himself. Luckily I was wrong. The matter has been taken care of."

He paused and I knew that was all he was going to say. Within thirty seconds he had flagged an acquaintance and started to move away. He turned back. "Give my best to Dennis."

I was ready to leave when Clive came in.

"I wanted to see you before I left. Thanks for stopping by." We shook hands like old friends.

"Mitch, you certainly know how to liven up a sleepy town. I haven't done so much criminal work in years.

"Your jail bunkmate has also been released. Seems his paperwork somehow disappeared and that is why he was held for so long."

"What's his story?"

Clive looked like he was going to object. A look I knew well.

"Career criminal or wrong place, wrong time?"

Clive thought for a moment. "Didn't make the right choice in women."

I nodded. "If he wants to hang around, tell him there's a job opening at the hardware store if he wants it. It will be up to him to keep it."

"You do this for all your jail buddies?"

I laughed. "What can I say? I just have a nose for the truth." I reached into my pocket and pulled out my card. "Can you send the bill for your services to the address on the card?"

Clive took the card and put it in his pants' pocket, then pulled an envelope out of his suit jacket. "I'm saving myself a stamp."

I opened the envelope and looked. The balance was zero. "It goes against my reporter instinct to accept services for free." We locked eyes each trying to get the upper hand.

I broke first. "How about if Clive Darrow makes a generous contribution to the Trudy Harrison Scholarship Fund?"

"I think that is a marvelous idea. Ever think of working in mediation, Mitch? You have the skills."

"Nope. My beat will always be crime."

We shook hands again and he left.

The crowd was beginning to thin as the clock approached nine. Sam came in and paid his respects and dropped something into the jar. I'd emailed him the information through Clive to make sure nothing could come back on me. I'd just buried the hatchet with Ram but wasn't sure how Sam would react. Sam played the room like a politician making sure he talked to everyone but not staying in any one group long.

Kim was busy stocking the bar, cutting up limes and lemons. He seemed filled with nervous energy as he darted back and forth. As I watched I began to see what the problem was. Kim was addicted. If I had to guess, it would be crack. All his profits and what he had taken from his dad were feeding his habit. After the energy phase, he would drop and need another fix. I just hoped the memorial was over before his personality changed. I'd seen that when I brought Trudy home. It was a Dr. Jekyll, Mr. Hyde syndrome. When he needed the drug he was unmerciful in his pursuit. Otherwise he was an okay guy.

I felt a little guilty knowing that this would be his last breath of freedom for ten to twenty years and the bar would be closed. Couldn't be helped. He would have to pay his debt to society. I didn't want Kim's drug problems to overshadow all that Trudy had accomplished.

I'd migrated to the bar to replace my beer with another cold one. Two was my limit tonight. Sam sat down on the barstool next to me. Kim was at the end of the bar talking to someone who was wiping tears from her eyes.

"It will be handled tonight after the last patron leaves."

I nodded. "I'm glad you let him do this for his sister. She would have approved."

Sam turned a little red, embarrassed by my statement and I couldn't help teasing him. "You will have this town cleaned up yet."

He cleared his throat and I thought I might have heard a single word about a part of my anatomy, but I could be wrong.

"Also wanted you to know the DEA agent is going to make it. He survived a second surgery. He's given us details in bits and snatches. He will be hospitalized for a couple of weeks and won't be back on the job for a couple of months. He said to say thanks."

I nodded. There was one more bit of information I needed to tell Sam. He had a dirty cop in his office.

"Sam, have you looked at your department for someone tipping off the dealers?"

He nodded. "I can't keep any secrets from the master reporter." He laughed. "I should have known better. Luke had already given his supervisor evidence on Wayne. I'd been watching him as well. He is no longer employed by the police department and is cooperating with the DEA to cut his sentence to little or nothing. He's ratting out everyone he can think of to get the best deal. Might even get witness protection."

I nodded then remembered I'd given Scoop a cryptic suggestion about a crooked police officer. "You may get an aggressive reporter in your office about that. Be nice."

Sam laughed. "Don't I know it? She's already scared half my officers. They will tell her anything to have her gone. Reminds me of another reporter I know."

I laughed at that and was glad Scoop was earning her own clips.

Sam moved on and so did I. I didn't need to be here to see Kim get arrested.

There was one more couple I needed to thank. "Harold and Kate, the display looks lovely. You really captured what Trudy was about through the photos."

"She was a beautiful girl. It's such a shame." Kate glanced at the entry table.

"Kate, Harold, I want to thank you for all you did to make my stay in Flatville bearable. It could have turned out much differently without you."

"Why don't we sit down?" Harold motioned to the booth I'd sat in earlier with Scott. I took one side and faced the pair.

Harold had something on his mind. "Mitch, I watched you grow up. You were a pretty normal kid until that poor boy died. Something of you died with him. Do you realize you never visited for cookies after that? We watched you grow but never mature. You became more introverted. I would be remiss in my friendship to your parents if I didn't say something."

What was he talking about? I get the pulling away part, but what did he expect? I nodded to keep him talking and hopefully soon he would make sense.

"We hope you'll return to Flatville. Lots of issues have been resolved. Maybe you can bury the hatchet with your cousin. I've talked to Monty and he would happily hire you to be the news editor. You could return to the community."

Flatville hadn't grown on me that much. I was Mitch Malone, ace reporter. I wasn't ready to turn in my notebook and settle for a desk job. There were still stories out there that needed to be covered and I was the best man for the job.

"I'll think about it but I like my job, where I live. I'm not ready to give up the big city life. Maybe in a few years."

Kate nodded. "It was worth a shot. You would be good for the community. Look at what you accomplished in less than a week. We understand, but when you are ready to move on, remember Flatville."

I nodded to signal I received the message. They got up and started working the room shaking, the last hands and giving hugs. They were the perfect host and hostess of this affair in Trudy's father's absence. I thought she'd approve.

I was antsy and wanted to get on the road. Time to return to Grand River.

The ghosts that had haunted me for years had dissipated. I wouldn't fear my childhood memories but embrace them. Five years would fly by and I looked forward to attending the next reunion.

The End

About the Author

W.S. GAGER has lived in Michigan for most of her life except when she was interviewing race car drivers or professional women golfers. She enjoyed the fast-paced life of a newspaper reporter until deciding to settle down and realized babies didn't adapt well to running down story details on deadline. Since then she honed her skills on other forms of writing before deciding to do what she always wanted with her life and that was to write mystery novels. Her main character in the award-winning Mitch Malone Mysteries is an edgy crime-beat reporter always on the hunt for the next Pulitzer.

CPSIA information can be obtained at www.ICGtesting.com
Printed in the USA
266347BV00002B/7/P

9 781610 090179